Perumal Murugan heads the department of Tamil literature at a government college in Attur, Tamil Nadu. He is the author of ten novels and five collections each of short stories and poems, as well as ten books of non-fiction. Several of his novels, stories and poems have been translated into English, including *Seasons of the Palm*, which was shortlisted for the Kiriyama Prize, *Current Show*, *One Part Woman* and *Pyre*. He has also written a memoir, *Nizhal Mutrattu Ninaivugal* (2013).

N. Kalyan Raman is a Chennai-based translator of Tamil fiction and poetry into English. He has published ten works of translated fiction and over two hundred poems by leading Tamil poets in journals and anthologies in India and abroad. In February 2017, he received the prestigious Pudumaipithan award, given by Vilakku, for his contribution to Tamil literature.

Praise for *Poonachi*

'*Poonachi* is a classic Perumal Murugan novel, empathetically illuminating lives of quiet dignity overrun by subjugation and hardship.' —*Livemint*

'Perumal Murugan's *Poonachi* offers a sharp, ironic take on society and the powers that be'. —*The Indian Express*

'The book is more than political criticism, Murugan explores eco-criticism and eco-feminism.' —*Business Standard*

'... Murugan once again gets behind the weak and the powerless. His new novel is at once a document of pain and suffering, and a strong statement.' —*Financial Express*

*

Jury Comments from the JCB prize of Literature:

'Funny and warm, *Poonachi* is a book that forces us gently to look at ourselves and our contribution to an unequal world. Perumal Murugan is a master story-teller who reflects profoundly on our transactional society and its inequities and struggles. Through the character of the lonely goat, he has written a powerful modern fable.'

- Longlisted for the DSC Prize for South Asian Literature 2018, Atta Galatta-Bangalore Lit Fest Book Prize for fiction, 2018 and The Hindu Prize 2018 for the best Indian literary fiction 2018.

- Longlisted for the Oxford Bookstore Book Cover Prize

POONACHI

OR THE STORY OF A BLACK GOAT

PERUMAL MURUGAN

TRANSLATED FROM THE TAMIL BY N. KALYAN RAMAN

cntxt

First published in hardback in 2018 by Context, an imprint of Westland Publications Private Limited

First published in paperback in 2019 by Context, an imprint of Westland Publications Private Limited

1st Floor, A Block, East Wing, Plot No. 40, SP Infocity, Dr. MGR Salai, Perungudi, Kandanchavadi, Chennai 600096

Westland, the Westland logo, Context and the Context logo, are the trademarks of Westland Publications Private Limited, or its affiliates.

Original Copyright © Perumal Murugan, 2018
Translation Copyright © N. Kalyan Raman, 2018

ISBN: 9789386850966

10 9 8 7 6 5 4

This is a work of fiction. Names, characters, organisations, places, events and incidents are either products of the author's imagination or used fictitiously.

Typeset in Garamond Premier Pro by SŪRYA, New Delhi
Printed at Manipal Technologies Limited, Manipal

The Dormant Seed

(Preface to the original Tamil edition of *Poonachi*,
published in December 2016)

HOW LONG CAN an untold story rest in deep slumber within
the dormant seed? I am fearful of writing about humans;
even more fearful of writing about gods. I can write about
demons, perhaps. I am even used to a bit of the demonic
life. I could make it an accompaniment here. All right, then,
let me write about animals.

There are only five species of animals with which I am
deeply familiar. Of them, dogs and cats are meant for poetry.
It is forbidden to write about cows or pigs. That leaves only
goats and sheep. Goats are problem-free, harmless and,
above all, energetic. A story needs narrative pace. Therefore,
I chose to write about goats.

I didn't take very long to write this novel. Three months
went by like a second. In that moment, pushing aside all
the confusions, dilemmas and sorrows I had experienced so
far, a great joy filled my being. The reason was Poonachi.
It was a major challenge to create her on the page and the
chief impediment was the diffidence that had come to reside

in me. I believed that Poonachi would be able to break it. Having finished the novel, I feel now that my faith in her was not unjustified.

To begin with, I had chosen a single title, 'The Story of a Black Goat' for this novel. In the course of writing, 'Poonachi' appeared unexpectedly. Then I tried to combine both titles. Most early Tamil novels of the last quarter of the nineteenth century had double titles of this kind. The original title of the first ever Tamil novel was *Pratapam ennum Pratapa Mudaliar Charithiram* (*Heroic Exploits*, or *The Story of Pratapa Mudaliar*). There are many other examples, such as *Abathukkidamana Abavatham alladhu Kamalambal Charithiram* (*Dangerous Slander*, or *The Story of Kamalambal*) and *Nalina Sundari alladhu Nagarigath Thadapudal* (*Graceful Damsel*, or *The Clamour of Modernity*). The present title has helped me realise my wish to place this novel, at least by virtue of its name, in the tradition of those distant forbears.

The number of people to whom I must express my gratitude is large. First on that list are my friend and Madurai high court lawyer G.R. Swaminathan, and his wife, Mrs Kamakshi Swaminathan. There is much that I have received from them. One day, I wrote in my diary, 'The unfortunate lesson that I've learnt from my experience of living all these years is that people are not that good or straight.' That same day, I met Swaminathan for the first time. In the two years that I've spent in his company, my opinion has changed completely. That you can go beyond ideological differences and bind people together with love is an important lesson that I learnt from him. The other person who had an equal impact on me and encouraged me to face everything with a smiling face was Mrs Kamakshi Swaminathan. I take great pleasure in dedicating this novel, which in a way can be considered my first work of prose fiction, to these two extraordinary individuals.

When I shared the title of the novel with my friend, Srinivasan Natarajan, he gave me his vote of confidence and cheered me on. I appreciate his hard work and enthusiasm in designing the covers of the various re-issues of my novels and thank him with all my heart.

My grateful thanks to everyone.

Perumal Murugan
Namakkal
24 December 2016

1

Once, in a village, there was a goat. No one knew where she was born. The birth of an ordinary life never leaves a trace, does it? That said, the goat's arrival into the world was somewhat unusual.

In that semi-arid stretch of land known as Odakkan Hill, it didn't rain much that year. The last few years had been no different. If it rained for half an hour on a rare day, some upstarts would call it 'torrential rain'. They had never seen a rainy season when it poured relentlessly throughout the day, for months on end. When it rained heavily, they cursed, 'Why is it pouring like this?' They were fed up of having to protect their possessions from the rain and getting drenched whenever they stepped out. But even an enemy should be welcomed with courtesy. If we curse and drive away the rain that brings us wealth and prosperity, why should it ever visit us again?

Pondering thus about the lack of rain, the old man sat on a hillock a short distance from his field and stared vacantly at the sky. He was a farmer who belonged to the community of Asuras. Harvesting had just been completed in all the fields. The yield was modest. But even after the

1

harvest, some grass lay green and lush in the fields. Soon, the season of dew would be here. The dew cover would help the grass withstand the sun's heat and survive for a few more days before drying up completely. Though the old man had a few goats that he could graze there, he wished he had one more goat that he could put to feed and raise in two short months.

There was a small pit below the hillock where he sat, beyond which lay a stretch of sun-baked fields. He loved to sit there at sunset and watch the spectacle of a crimson blanket spreading over the horizon. On the days when he grazed his goats there, as well as on some other days, he would leave only after watching the colourful spectacle unfold in the sky. If he happened to miss it, he would feel aggrieved, as though he had been robbed of something precious. 'Sit in the field and gaze at the sky for some time. It will clear your mind,' the old man's wife would tease him.

One day, while he was enjoying the sunset, an unusual sight on the long foot trail adjoining the field caught his eye. A very large silhouette was moving in the far distance. It looked as if a tree trunk shorn of all branches had uprooted itself and was walking on the trail. The old man stood up instinctively. In the next few moments, it became obvious that what he was looking at was the figure of a man, elongated in the light of dusk.

The old man knew everyone in the area, even the local children of all ages. Who could this be? He couldn't tell from the gait. In the space between one giant step and the next, he thought, a six-foot-tall man could lie down and extend his arms freely on either side.

It was the hour of dusk, and the figure was moving quickly, perhaps because he wanted to reach somewhere before nightfall. It seemed that he would pass by this spot in a few more seconds. The old man believed that there wasn't a soul in the region that he didn't know. He had also never imagined that it would be so easy for someone to ignore him and walk away. Who was this giant?

Some moments later, the swinging movement of his right hand and his bent left arm came into view. When he saw that the giant was holding his left arm against his chest, the old man wondered if he perhaps had no use of that arm. If he picked up that much speed by swinging a lone arm, imagine how fast he could go if he swung his left arm too! To try to find out who the giant might be, the old man climbed down towards the trail.

The giant was an imposing figure, half as tall as a palm tree, wearing just a loincloth at his waist. The cloth seemed to flutter in the breeze. Though the old man had spotted him from afar, the giant had drawn near in no time. It looked as if he would race past the spot and be gone forever in a couple of seconds. Afraid that he might slip by, the old man shouted from a distance: 'Who goes there?' At once the giant stopped in his tracks. 'It's me, samiyov,' he called out. His voice sounded like a wasp burrowing through a block of wood. The old man still couldn't recognise him. Though he was still at a distance, he had to look up to see the giant's face.

'Who are you? You seem to be new around here,' the old man said.

'Not at all,' the giant replied. 'I belong to this area. I am wandering from village to village, trying to sell this goat kid. I haven't found a buyer yet. She is just a day-old baby. That's why I am going to every field, samiyov.'

'If you go to the market fair, she'll be sold in no time,' the old man said.

'Who will buy my baby at a market fair, sami?' the giant laughed.

This one is very arrogant, thought the old man.

'The fellows will come, one by one, hold her jaw and look at her teeth. They'll clasp her waist with their fingers, pull at her udder and stroke her back. Haven't we seen the poor goats standing around like showpieces at market fairs? Would I let any old hand touch this precious baby? That's why I couldn't bring myself to take her to a market fair. Raising this baby goat and making a living from it is beyond me. So I am roaming from village to village, trying to find someone who will look after her properly,' the giant explained.

Seems like this giant's tongue, too, will stretch as long as his body, the old man thought. He glanced at the kid. She was scarcely visible. Maybe she was resting comfortably in the crook of his arm. In the fading light of dusk, he couldn't see her clearly. He was reluctant to step closer.

'You say you went to several villages. Did no one there have the money to buy this wonder kid?'

'Oh, men of fortune are as plentiful as fruit worms, but

a kind heart is rare. Only a kind-hearted man can have my baby,' the giant said.

He bent down and set the kid on the ground. His back was as broad as a slab of granite. A big, fat worm wriggled near his feet. Standing upright again, he took off his head-towel and wiped the sweat from his face and upper body.

'Look, she is no ordinary kid. Her mother birthed seven kids in a litter. After she delivered the sixth, I thought it was all over and only the umbilical cord would be left. But she contracted her body and pushed hard once more. This one slid out as the seventh and dropped like a piece of dung. She is truly a miracle, look at her,' the giant said.

A pleasant breeze had crept in at sunset, but sweat streamed down the giant's torso like a rivulet. The old man looked on in surprise as he stemmed the flow with his towel and wiped himself dry. 'What kind of man is he? Is he from a different planet?' he mused, while the giant continued: 'I can't wander around anymore, sami. My days are at an end. I'll hand over this kid to you and move on. Keep her under your care, samiyov.'

He lifted the kid and placed her in the old man's hands. At first, it felt as if a hammer had grazed his hand; the next moment, he found a flower on his palm. The old man had never seen such a tiny goat kid before. He gazed at her in amazement. Her wriggling form fit snugly into the crook of his arm. The kid's colour was all black, the shiny black of a beetle. With his palm resting on her throat, he looked up. The giant was gone, fading into the darkness at the end of the trail.

'Yov, yov! Don't you want money for the kid?' the old man shouted. The giant couldn't have heard him. The old man stood still and watched as the figure dwindled to a speck and then vanished altogether. As he turned back slowly, the old man was gripped by anxiety. He had wished for a goat to graze on the green grass. By chance, this bit of dung had come into his hands. How was he going to raise it to adulthood?

2

THE OLD MAN climbed the hillock and stepped into the field. He had plucked some grass and filled a basket with it. After laying the kid on the bed of grass, he lifted the basket and placed it on his head, and started walking. Arriving as a smoky haze, darkness had begun to settle slowly across the crimson sky in the west. It was time to head homeward. Someone like that giant, with his long strides, would probably have got there in no time.

The old man's thatched shed was at a walking distance from the field. He had to go past the field, take the mud track, then cross the lake shore and trudge along the very long foot trail that wound through the stretch of semi-arid fields in order to reach home.

By the time he got on the foot trail, his shadow had begun to fade. He took long strides, hurrying to reach home before it was too dark to see ahead. There were shorn fields all across the stretch. Here and there, he saw a few men who were taking their goats back home after grazing them on the new grass. But for this goat kid, he would have been home by now with the basket of grass.

As he walked on, he suddenly heard the kid cry out again and again, like a steady hum. This worm of a kid had not only eaten up his time, she was now crying; he scolded her. Then he saw a bunch of goatherds come running towards him from all four directions, yelling, 'Dhooyi, dhooyi.' The old man stopped in his tracks, sensing that something was amiss. A gust of wind seemed to be pushing the basket off his head. He held on to it tightly. A man rushed forward, caught the old man by the arm and steadied him. Otherwise, he would have fallen face down in the dirt. He lifted the basket off the old man's head and kept it on the ground. After recovering his wits, the old man asked breathlessly, 'What's happening?'

'Look over there,' the man said, pointing to the west. Flapping its wings, a large bird was flying away towards the hill where it was already dark.

'What do you have in the basket that a large bird would hunt?' Two or three men approached him with the question. 'Is it a rat that you caught in the field?'

Meanwhile, the kid stood up slowly inside the basket and moaned: 'Mmmm.' Still shaken, the old man was unable to speak.

'You had this big black worm in the basket. That's why the eagle struck,' laughed one man as he picked up the kid.

'This is a goat kid, 'pa,' said another.

The kid wriggled like a worm in the hands of the man who had picked it up. All the goatherds looked at it in wonder. 'Is she really a goat kid?'

They took her in their hands and examined her. The old man was embarrassed. If the goatherds had not spotted the eagle swooping down on the basket, it would have snatched the kid in its talons and eaten her.

'Look at the kid. This moment of peril must have been in her destiny,' the old man thought to himself. Then he addressed the goatherds: 'Like providence, you people turned up at the right time to help me. On top of losing the kid, I might have taken a fall with the basket and broken a limb. What would I have done then? There's my wife at home. She feeds me every day because I do a little work and earn something. If I am laid up in bed with a broken limb, would she look after me?'

A goatherd in a loincloth held the kid in his hand and said, 'Her belly is empty, 'pa. Look at her. She is so hungry she can't even open her eyes.' He called out, 'Bu-ck-oo, bu-ck-oo' and his goats came running to him. He picked a nanny goat and held the kid under her udder. The kid was too weak to reach for the udder, so he crammed the nanny goat's teat into her mouth. It was perhaps the first time the kid was trying to hold a teat in her mouth. After a bit of a struggle, she managed to hold it firmly and sucked on it. When the first drops of milk touched her tongue, she discovered a new taste and began to suckle eagerly.

'The kid is quite smart,' said the man who had arranged to feed her. After a few sucks had drenched her belly, her jaw began to ache and the kid let go of the teat. 'Go on, drink a little more. It'll make sure that you pass the night without hunger pangs,' the young man said and made her suckle some more. Then he picked her up and handed her over to the old man. 'She looks like a worm, but with her attitude, she is already an adult,' he said.

The men set out behind their herds. After placing the kid safely inside the basket and covering her with grass, the old man started walking on the trail. 'I don't know how many more hazards this creature will have to face. Will she overcome them or go under? Who knows what is fated for her?' he mused.

The old woman didn't like the look or sound of the kid. She scowled at her husband. 'Where did you pick up this kitten? Why do we need her?' When the old man told her she was a goat kid, she picked her up and exclaimed in amazement: 'Yes, she *is* a goat kid.'

All night, they went over the story of how the kid had come into their hands. They already owned two goats. One of them had littered just a month ago. Three kids: two male and one female. All three jumped and played around in their front yard. The other goat was pregnant and would deliver about a month from now. They had sold the kids from her previous litter to the butcher only ten days ago. They also owned a buffalo calf, a heifer. If she grazed for another year, she would be old enough to mate, and then they could sell her.

The couple spent their days raising a few crops in the half acre of land adjoining their thatched shed, grazing their goats and tending the buffalo calf. It fell to the old man to take the goats to the fields for grazing and fetch fodder for the goats and the calf. Using that as an excuse, he liked to wander across the fields and villages, bantering with people and enjoying a few laughs. His wife rarely went out anywhere. Since their needs were very few, she went to the market fair once a month to buy groceries. They also visited their daughter's home once a year for the annual festival at the village temple, which involved being away for a fortnight. She was their only daughter, and they had no other wish than to pass the remainder of their lives as serenely as they had done all these years.

That same night the old lady gave the goat kid that resembled a kitten a nickname: Poonachi. She once had a cat by the same name. In memory of that beloved cat, this goat kid too was named Poonachi. They had acquired her without spending a penny. Now they had to look after her somehow. Her husband had told her a vague story about meeting a demon who looked like Bakasuran and receiving the kid from him as a gift. She wondered if he could have stolen it from a goatherd. Someone might come looking for it tomorrow. Maybe her husband had told her the story only to cover up his crime?

The old woman was not used to lighting lamps at night. The couple ate their evening meal and went to bed when it was still dusk. That night, though, she took a large earthen lamp and filled it with castor oil extracted the year before. There was no cotton for a wick. She tore off a strip from a discarded loincloth of her husband's and fashioned it into a wick.

She looked at the kid under the lamplight in that shed as though she were seeing her own child after a long time apart. There was no bald spot or bruise anywhere on her body. The kid was all black. As she stared at the lamp, her wide open eyes were starkly visible. There was a trace of fatigue on her face. The old woman thought the kid looked haggard because she had not been fed properly. She must be just a couple of days old. A determination that she must somehow raise this kid to adulthood took root in her heart.

She called the old man to come and see the kid. She looked like a black lump glittering in the lamplight in that pitch-black night. He pulled fondly at her flapping ears and said, 'Aren't you lucky to come and live here?'

It had been a long time since there was such pleasant chit-chat between the couple. Because of the kid's sudden entry into their lives, they ended up talking about the old days.

12

3

SINCE THE GOATHERD on the trail had got his nanny goat to suckle her, the kid's belly was full. Around midnight the old woman started feeling sleepy. Folding a gunny bag into a small square and spreading it on the ground like a mattress, she laid the kid on it and covered her with an upside-down basket. Bewildered by the darkness inside the basket, the kid cried a little, but didn't come out. Since the basket was coated with dung, she couldn't find even a small opening anywhere. The basket's edge sat flush on the gunny bag. Concerned that the kid might not have any air to breathe, the old woman brought a stick of firewood, placed it on one side and raised the edge on it. Now there was enough room for air to circulate.

The kid slept right below the old woman's cot. The old woman got up every now and then, lifted the basket, and looked at the kid. Curled up on the gunny bag mattress, the little thing lay fast asleep.

A couple of hours after midnight, when the woman opened the basket to check, the kid struggled to her feet and cried out. Contracting her body a bit, she peed. 'Poonachi, how will you sleep if your bed is damp?' the old woman asked as she hurriedly pulled the kid out. But once she was out, Poonachi circled the old woman's legs, bleating plaintively; sucking on an ankle, she tried to feed.

'Is your stomach troubling you, Poonachi?' the old woman asked and picked up the kid. She went to the hut where the goats were tied up for the night. The nanny goat which had recently delivered her litter was lying on the ground, chewing the cud. The old woman roused her. Thinking that she was about to get something to eat, the goat stood up eagerly and tugged at the woman's waist.

As if they had been waiting for that moment, three kids came running and attacked the nanny goat's udder. Two kids grabbed hold of a teat each. The third tried hard to push the others aside with its snout to also grab a teat. Their bodies trembled as they suckled fiercely. Holding Poonachi in her hand, the old woman didn't know what to do. She thought of waking the old man. He had fallen into a deep slumber just moments earlier. Otherwise, given the din the kids were making, he would have got up by now and yelled at them.

Forcefully pushing aside the kid who sat beside the nanny goat with the teat on the near side in its mouth, she brought Poonachi's mouth closer. Poonachi's nostrils must have sensed the odour of milk. Immediately, she tried to catch the teat in her mouth. Because the goat's own kids had suckled on it, the teat had become swollen and was too big for Poonachi's mouth. So she caught a tip between her lips and tugged at it. The milk tasted even better than when she had been suckled earlier that day, and Poonachi went at it avidly.

She didn't have the energy to butt the udder. The old woman didn't release her hold either. Had Poonachi stood on the ground, the udder would have been beyond her reach. Just when she had wet her belly to some extent, the realisation that an infant's tender mouth was pressed around her teat dawned on the goat. Kicking her legs, she changed her position. Even then, her kids pushed their heads at her udder and continued to suckle.

'Oh, you caught on to her quickly, eh?' the old woman said as she patted the goat on her head. Then, holding a hind leg of the goat with one hand, she let Poonachi, whom she was holding in her other hand, suckle the goat. The nanny goat knew the feeding style of her kids. She tried to protect her udder from the intruder by jumping and sliding around.

Every now and then, when his body became overheated, the old man would ask for goat's milk. His wife would tie up the kids and squeeze a tumbler of milk from the goat's udder early in the morning before letting them out to feed. The old man would receive the tumbler of raw milk in his hand and pour it into his mouth. On some days, he would ask her to boil it. She would drop a bit of palm jaggery in the boiled milk and give it to him. The milk and the eats made from it didn't agree with the old woman. She drank it rarely, and reluctantly.

For the nanny goat, it was a new experience to suckle a kid other than her own. She had to fight to protect her udder. In the ensuing mêlée, Poonachi's belly got half-filled. Stroking the tiny stomach, the old woman said, 'Right. You've had enough for now. Go to sleep. We'll take care of it in the morning,' and put her back under the basket. Now that Poonachi had got a taste of milk, she couldn't control her craving. Instead of lying down under the cover of the basket, she butted it again and again, and tried to suckle, until she finally became exhausted and lay down to sleep.

The same thing happened over the next few days. Sometimes the old man came along to assist his wife. With one of them holding the goat's neck in a firm grip and the other holding its legs together, they would get Poonachi to suckle. The goat didn't at all wish to suckle this kid. She would try to break free and run. But the old woman wouldn't give up. The moment she woke the goat to suckle Poonachi, all her three kids would come running. Pushing them away was hard. When all three of them butted the goat's udder, inserting Poonachi in the middle was difficult too. She couldn't put them inside a basket either. If she tried to get Poonachi to suckle while the kids were away nibbling grass in the pasture, the goat would raise her voice and call out to her kids. Wherever they might be, the kids would come leaping and running as soon as they heard their mother's call.

Somehow, on most days, Poonachi got enough milk to fill half, or at least a quarter, of her stomach. At this rate, how would she ever recover and grow up healthy? If only she could manage for a month, she could start eating grass and leaves. The old woman worried about it all the time. For his part, the old man would tell her, 'She comes from a line that can deliver a litter of seven. Some fellow turned up from nowhere like God and gifted her to me. Don't treat her like an orphan.' Whenever she was unable to get the goat to suckle Poonachi, she would fling random abuse at him: 'The old wretch has brought this kitten home only to take the life out of me.'

But there was a problem in getting even the small quantity of milk that kept Poonachi alive. The nanny goat had learnt the skill of making its udder go dry at will. If they tried to get Poonachi to suckle when her kids were not around, no milk would flow from her teats. If she let Poonachi in when the kids were suckling, the teat simply would not yield another drop. The goat would contract her body and retract the teat. While suckling her own kids, she would tilt her head upward, close her eyes, drool at the mouth and stand still as she happily chewed the cud. The old woman would watch as the goat splayed her legs and suckled her kids at her softened udder. Shaking their tails, which were no bigger than the old woman's little finger, the kids would keep at it. Only after her udder was completely empty would she part from her kids and walk away.

'Come on, woman, who told you not to suckle your own kids? Do it like a queen, who can stop you? This Poonachi is a living creature too. The poor thing is starving, can't you see? What do you lose if you feed her a little milk so that she can survive? Your kids are foraging in the pasture, aren't they? This Poonachi is not going to take away your abundance, is she? Don't you have even a little bit of compassion?' the old woman would lament.

The goat would stare at her as if she didn't understand a thing. 'You can feign a dry udder whenever you want, but you don't understand what I am saying? I know you're just pretending,' the old woman would say.

In spite of all the coaxing, the old woman's attempts to get the deceitful goat – Kalli – to suckle Poonachi were of no avail. Poonachi couldn't get even a small fraction of the nourishment she needed. The old woman was afraid that at this rate, her guts would shrivel up and she would meet a horrible end. She didn't really believe that Poonachi was of a line that delivered a litter of seven every time. But a man had gifted her to them like a boon from God. He had trusted them to look after her. When passing that way after a few months, if he suddenly remembered Poonachi and came by to look her up, what would they tell him? Could they bring themselves to say that she had died of starvation? If they couldn't fill the belly of such a tiny creature, what was the point of living?

Though she didn't need to go to the market fair that week, the old woman set out nevertheless. Her main task was to buy a feeding tube with which she could get some nourishing liquid into the kid. She found a feeding bottle and two tubes. If one were to tear, she could use the other.

Once she returned from the market, she took the pot in which cooked millet had been left to soak overnight and drained the water from it, then poured the water into the bottle and fixed the feeding tube around its mouth. Keeping Poonachi on her lap, she crammed the feeding tube into the kid's mouth. At first, the kid was perplexed. Once some milk-like liquid had trickled in, she grabbed the tube with her mouth and began to suckle. It wasn't milk, only bland-tasting rice water. After swallowing a couple of mouthfuls, she pulled away from the tube.

The old woman wouldn't let her go. She fed Poonachi little by little and was satisfied only when she saw that her belly was swollen and full. Poonachi found it hard to walk with her bloated belly. She stood in the same spot for some time, then lay down. From then on, she was fed the water from cooked millet rice or paste three or four times a day. Occasionally, she was able to get a few squirts of milk from the nanny goat. For Poonachi, the milk was a rare treat.

Since she grew up on rice water, Poonachi's belly was always bloated. The hair on her body began to look matted. She had to survive this phase somehow, that was all that mattered. Her health would pick up, though it might take a few months. Once she was old enough to forage for food on her own, she would gradually recover. What she needed now was some fluid to keep her alive, and rice water was adequate for that.

Poonachi practised taking feeble steps towards the front yard and the goat shed. But Kalli's kids simply couldn't stand the sight of her. Fed on a plentiful diet of mother's milk, their hips had become hard and plump, endowing them with a natural swagger. They jumped and leapt about all the time.

19

Climbing the tall mortar that stood in the front yard and jumping off it was their favourite sport. They also enjoyed playfully butting one another with their hornless heads. Now and again, the old woman would scold them and bring them to order. But their cavorting continued without restraint. As Poonachi walked past them looking like a lifeless doll, they would come running and sniff her all over. They would butt her with their bald heads and knock her down. Poonachi would cry in a feeble voice. The more she cried, the more high-spirited they became. They would raise a foreleg and rest it on her back. They thought up many kinds of games to torment Poonachi.

Even as Poonachi trembled and contracted her body in fear, the kids would run towards her, leapfrog over her body and stand on the other side – this was one game. As the three of them jumped over her, one after the other, a whirring sound assailed her ears. Poonachi would tremble and shrink in fear, and let out a high-pitched wail.

Sometimes, when Poonachi was stretched out either in the front yard or on the gunny bag under the old woman's cot, the kids would approach her with feigned affection and lie down next to her, with their heads resting on her body. Poonachi would feel suffocated. She would try very hard to get up and move away. But where could she find the strength to lift those big heads and push them aside? Her only hope was that they would recognise her distress and get up on their own. Whenever she saw them, she would become petrified and seek refuge between the old woman's legs. The old woman would chase them away and protect her.

The goats were far better behaved than the kids. If Poonachi went near Kalli, she would bring her head down and smell the kid, then give her a slight push. She had long, curved horns – not that they were of much use. She could only butt with her bald head, her way of saying, 'Go away!'

The other nanny goat would look protectively at Poonachi. When she rubbed her face against Poonachi, it felt as if her own mother was caressing her. Even if Poonachi lay down next to her, she would do nothing to discourage the kid. Only when Poonachi reached for her udder, not realising that she was pregnant, did she get annoyed. She would lift a hind leg and move away; she would also warn Poonachi with a mild grunt: 'Don't try such tricks with me.'

And so, Poonachi stayed alive by drinking rice water three times a day and occasionally a little milk. She was confined inside the basket at night. During the day she lay around in the shed, in the front yard, or inside the hut. When the old woman took the goats out for grazing, she carried Poonachi in her arms. In the fields, she would walk between the old woman's legs. This was how Poonachi grew up day by day. Fifteen days had passed since she had first arrived.

One day, another old woman, a relative, came to visit. She stayed overnight in the couple's shed. The women sat talking late into the night about the old days. The old man placed his cot near the goats' hut. Both women brought their cots to the front yard and stretched out on them. It was a night of the waning crescent moon and pitch black. Their chit-chat was nowhere near winding down. Many stories of a bygone time came up. Both of them fell asleep, open-mouthed, in the course of their conversation.

That night the old woman forgot all about Poonachi. She didn't put the kid inside the basket. Poonachi called out a few times, but the old woman didn't hear her. Poonachi had no idea where to sleep. She wondered whether she should go to the hut and sleep next to the nanny goat. If the goat rolled over in the dark, Poonachi could be trapped and crushed under her body. It had almost happened a few times. She was also afraid to walk from the front yard into the dark night. So she lay down on a bed of dung dirt under the old woman's cot. The rice water was very sour that day. Poonachi had liked the taste very much. When fresh, it tasted as bland as plain water. Tonight, she had drunk a lot more than she normally did. Her belly was tight as a fist.

As if in a dream, she felt something seize her throat. Involuntarily, she let out a loud cry. It was the loudest she had cried yet. The old woman got up from her cot, shouting 'Dhooyi, dhooyi!' She picked up the stick she had placed near the cot and ran in the direction of the sound. The moon had just appeared in the sky. In the dim light, she saw a strange creature running away with Poonachi in its grip. After that one scream, Poonachi's throat had choked up. She realised that her neck was caught between two rows of sharp teeth. She couldn't make out a thing.

The old woman raised her arm and hurled the stick in her hand. It smashed into the creature's back, bounced off and fell away. Staggering from the unexpected blow, the creature lost its hold on Poonachi, and she fell to the ground and rolled over two or three times. The creature could not locate her immediately. By then, the old woman had come menacingly close, shouting 'dhooyi, dhooyi'. The creature decided to flee for dear life. Since there was no prey in its mouth, it ran away at great speed.

Hearing no sound, the old woman stopped in her tracks. Unable to rise to her feet, Poonachi cried in a feeble voice. Though it sounded no louder than a blade of grass being ripped, the old woman heard it. She came to the spot and groped in the dark for Poonachi. Meanwhile, the crescent moon had climbed a little higher and there was some light. The old woman scooped up Poonachi from the ground and brought her to the shed. The old man and the guest had woken up too and asked her, 'What happened? What happened?' After thrusting Poonachi into the old man's hands, the old woman ran inside the house. The lamp she had lit on the night Poonachi came home still had the wick in it. When she came out with it, the old man had Poonachi on his lap and was stroking her fondly. In the lamplight, they saw the tooth marks embedded on either side of Poonachi's neck. While the marks were light on one side, they had sunk deep on the other and blood was pouring out of the wound.

Near the place where she washed utensils, the old woman had planted a shrub of coatbuttons, a medicinal plant. She ran there, plucked a few leaves, crushed them and applied the extract on the wound. To Poonachi, who was numb from shock and pain, the burning sensation produced by the leaf extract brought some clarity. Unable to bear the pain, she screamed aloud. Their guest asked the old man, 'Do you think the kid will pull through?'

'I go to sleep every night only after putting her in the basket. Today I dozed off, lost in the pleasure of our conversation. They talk about the highs of toddy and liquor, but those are not highs at all. Real intoxication comes from talking. The moment it crosses a limit, we forget everything,' the old woman lamented.

'You did run and catch hold of her somehow. But did you find out who or what came to snatch her?' her husband asked.

4

POONACHI HERSELF WAS clueless about the creature that had tried to snatch her away. The way she had been grabbed by the neck, with her body suspended in the air, felt like something out of a dream. It couldn't have been a dog. A dog was incapable of sneaking in at night and snatching anything. It could have been a jackal. But a jackal was unlikely to grab such a tiny kid. There were three other kids, bigger and fleshier than Poonachi, lying in the hut. The jackal would have targeted them. And a domestic cat hunts no bigger prey than a rat. This must have been a wildcat. Some villagers had seen wildcats roaming near the fields. Unable to find any prey, some of them might have strayed into the farmlands. Once they grabbed a goat and got a taste of the meat, no one would be able to control them.

There was a time when the couple had kept a dog. The last one they had owned was really smart. Its vigilant eyes wouldn't let even a fly or an ant trespass inside the shed. But the dog ate as much food as a grown man. It was a struggle trying to feed two mouths, how could they afford a third?

When the rainfall decreased and the yield went down

too, year after year, having an additional mouth to feed had to be a burden. But Poonachi escaped somehow. An eagle had tried to grab her the other day, and now this wildcat.

'This Poonachi will survive anything,' the old woman declared proudly. Stroking the kid's neck and back, she laid it next to her on the cot.

The next day, people from the village started streaming towards the shed right from the morning. The village had a very large number of goats and cattle. People depended on them for their livelihood. When they heard that some unknown creature had sneaked in to grab a goat kid, everyone was scared. People queued up to express their concern. Ten years ago, the whole village had turned up at the couple's shed for their daughter's wedding. After that, nobody had felt the need nor had the time to look them up. And now a goat kid had brought them all this attention.

Most people looked at Poonachi and burst out laughing.

'Where did you find this kid, ayah?'

'Will she ever grow up?'

'She is always crawling on the floor, like a pup mouse.'

'Don't tell me the wildcat trekked all the way for this puny creature?' they asked, surprised.

Everyone had the same concern: if they could know for certain whether it was a jackal or a wildcat, they could keep their goats safe from attack. After looking at the wounds on Poonachi's neck, everyone came up with their own ideas. In the end, they all agreed that it must have been a wildcat. A few men planned to trap it with a snare. Remembering the taste of wildcat meat, when baked and rolled into a round ball like the shell of a palmyra fruit, some old men clucked their tongues with relish. They declared that no other meat tasted so good, thereby stoking everyone's appetite. No doubt the snares lying in people's attics would be brought down and there would soon be a flurry of activity in the village.

'Do you feed the kid milk from a nanny goat?' asked a woman who owned a lone goat.

'Where do I go for milk, ayah? I manage to get her a couple of mouthfuls from that mother goat. But if Poonachi goes anywhere near her, she kicks her leg and moves away. So all three times of the day, I feed her the same rice water that we drink, but through a bottle.'

'Ayah ... when you go to the market fair, buy a kilo of coconut oilcake, soak it in water and make the kid drink it. She will become strong enough to stand on her own feet,' the goat-owner said.

Even though she had handled goats for a very long time, the old woman had never had the experience of bringing up a lone kid without a mother. How did I not think of this coconut oilcake, she asked herself. She decided that she would go to the market fair the very next week and buy some oilcake. It was not a big expense, really. If she bought and stored a kilo and a half, it would last for months. If she soaked a small round piece of oilcake as big as an areca nut, it would be enough for one meal. At other times of the day, the kid could be fed rice water as usual.

A woman laid Poonachi on her lap and stroked her, then lifted her ears and looked at them in wonder. Ears that stood up to the height of a middle finger and then folded down were new to her. Though the kid was puny, her ears were really long.

'So rare to find a kid whose colour is pitch black like this one, ayah. There are plenty of white and brown goats around. Rarely do we get to see a black goat. What you've got here is a miracle. Why haven't you got her ear pierced yet?'

Only then did the old man and his wife remember that they had to get the ear-piercing done. They panicked. They would normally buy goat kids at the market fair only after ensuring that their ears had been pierced. But Poonachi was a foundling on the trail and they had forgotten all about the requirement. Just a month and a half ago, they had got the ears of all the three kids of their nanny goat pierced, and had a hard time getting it done. If they took Poonachi to the authorities now, what would those big shots say?

The old man and his wife pondered the problem late into the night. How could they get Poonachi's ear pierced? It was a procedure prescribed by the regime. The regime itself arranged for the ear-piercing of its citizens and their pet animals. When a new creature was born anywhere in the territory controlled by the government, the authorities had to be informed immediately. All children and domestic animals had to get their ears pierced. After registering the details of name, age and address, the government would organise the ear-piercing. It had to be done within one month after birth.

Events like death and sale-purchase also had to be registered, but that was not a problem. Those were ordinary, routine matters. Ear-piercing wasn't like that. There would be a big crowd. The authorities would ask questions. All the information had to be correct. If the case was rejected because something was incorrect, the matter became complicated. To get it rectified, one had to run from pillar to post, chasing various officials. Even at the market fair, only kids with their ears pierced were sold or bought. Lost in the excitement of receiving Bakasuran's gift, the couple had forgotten all about getting Poonachi's ears pierced.

5

THE MAIN PROBLEM with getting Poonachi's ear pierced was the set of questions it would provoke. 'Where was she born? What was her mother's name? Who raised her mother? How much was she bought for?' The couple who owned Poonachi would have to respond to such questions. If they replied that they had received the newborn as a gift, that a man who looked like the gluttonous demon Bakasuran, had given her away, the authorities might register a case of false testimony.

'Bring that Bakasuran here,' they would say. 'Has he got his ear pierced? He could be a spy from a foreign country; are you his accomplice?'

Accusations would be flung at the couple like arrows. 'If he was in possession of a kid whose ears were not pierced, he might be an enemy of the regime,' the authorities would declare. If they were to ask, 'How did you come into contact with him? What else have you received from him?' the couple would have no answer. The regime had the power to turn its own people, at any moment, into adversaries, enemies and traitors.

After taking everything into account, they decided to wait for ten or fifteen days. In that time, the pregnant goat in their yard would have delivered her litter. Her first pregnancy had yielded just one kid; the next few uniformly yielded two kids each. They could easily club Poonachi with two newborns and claim a litter of three. Her puny shape would support that claim. Her black colour was a problem, however. Most of the goats in the state were white. A few were brown, but black ones were rare. Once upon a time, so the lore went, the state teemed with black goats. Since they could not be recognised in the dark when engaged in any criminal activity, the regime had, it was rumoured, deliberately wiped them out. Even so, black goats could still be spotted here and there. Their colour provoked instant hostility. When they saw Poonachi, the officials would go on the alert immediately.

From that day on, Poonachi got a reduced quantity of even the thin gruel she had to live on. The old woman was intent on not letting her grow fat. They would take the kids to the authorities four or five days after the pregnant goat delivered her litter. At that time, there should be no visible difference between Poonachi and the other two newborn kids. The old woman had deferred the idea of feeding Poonachi oilcake water. Even the spot where Poonachi usually slept at night was changed. She was locked up inside the goat hut. The old woman kept a wooden stick on her basket for extra protection.

For a few nights following the raid in which Poonachi

31

had been nearly carried away by a wildcat, the old man and his wife didn't sleep a wink. They expected the wildcat to come again. When one of them caught a nap for a few minutes, the other stayed awake. Fortunately, old people don't need more than a few hours of sleep.

Poonachi had become frightened of the dark. Even though she was caged inside the shed, she felt reassured only when she heard the old woman's voice. She had a recurring dream of hanging from the maw of a grotesque figure, and often wailed aloud unexpectedly.

The old woman took a vow of supplication to Mesagaran, their clan deity. 'If this Poonachi reaches puberty and has a litter, the first male kid will be yours, Mesayya,' she vowed.

Eleven days after the wildcat had tried to snatch Poonachi away, their nanny goat delivered her litter: two kids, just as they had expected. Both were male. Male kids were always somewhat robust at birth; the females turned out a little weak. If they claimed that Poonachi was born after the two kids, the authorities might believe them. The couple were pleased with the situation.

The two kids started jumping about and playing from the day they were born. It was decided that all three would be taken to the authorities on the third day to get their ears pierced. The old man was usually eager to step out of the house, but this time he told his wife, 'I can't do it. You go ahead.' She didn't try and compel him. How could a lone woman take a nanny goat and three kids all by herself? How would she manage once she reached there? But who else was there to accompany her anyway? She had no option but to suffer the ordeal, so she set out alone from her village.

Before she left, she made sure that the two kids were well fed by their mother. They were tender newborns; once they were fed, they went to sleep. She put Poonachi in the basket with them. She also kept the food container in the basket, covered with a cloth to keep the kids from toppling it.

She started before sunrise when it was still dark. Since the nanny goat was used to the old woman, there was no problem: she went along wherever she was led. Every now and then, she would cry out for the kids. If the kids responded with a cry from inside the basket, it was enough to appease the nanny goat. She walked on quietly. At dawn, the old woman had fed her a bunch of groundnut leaves and filled her belly too. With the basket on her head and the nanny goat in tow, the old woman crossed the fields, reached the road and continued her trek.

The ear-piercing office was three miles from their home. When the old woman arrived there, she found a very big crowd waiting ahead of her. She couldn't tell exactly how many people there were, but somehow she found herself a spot in the queue. She had to be vigilant and watch out for anyone trying to join the line out of turn. Whenever someone approached a person ahead of her, she suspected that they might be trying to infiltrate the queue. She was suspicious of them all. The officers were expected to arrive only at ten o'clock. If she had arrived later, she would have been pushed further back in the queue. Even so, she could see that her work might not be done that day. If she actually managed to get a token in her hand, she could be confident of being finished before nightfall. She could start the next morning and make her way slowly back to the village.

Some people who were ahead of her in the queue had sheep with them. Since sheep deliver only one lamb at a time, their work was done quickly. The old woman assessed the situation. There were about a dozen goats and a lot of sheep ahead of her in the queue. Most of the people happened to be familiar faces. She sat down in the queue and chatted with them. When the sun had climbed a little higher, she mashed some soft rice into gruel and drank it up. Since she would need to eat at least twice more, she made sure that she ate just enough to quench her hunger and had a sufficient amount left over. She lifted the kids out of the basket and set them down. They were suckled by the nanny goat. Enlisting the help of a girl beside her, she made sure that Poonachi also got a couple of feeds.

The girl asked, 'Isn't she the goat's kid?'

'Yes, she is, but the mother won't look at her, it seems.' Some nanny goats had the tendency to ignore their own kids and push them away. The old woman used this fact to her advantage.

As time went by, the queue grew longer and longer. The office compound was in a state of permanent uproar with the bleating of goats and the endless chatter of those waiting. There was a hullaballoo when some people entered the queue in the middle, claiming that they had reserved their spots earlier. A couple of men from the office came out and warned the noise-makers, then led them to the back of the queue. They also arranged for some who were at the back to go up to the front. No one could question what they were doing. They would simply say, 'The officer told us to bring them in.' Moreover, these men would pick on whoever dared to ask questions, purposely delay the work when their turn came and give them the run-around. It was clear that the work would proceed only if those who were waiting held their peace and behaved humbly with the officials.

Everyone was well versed in how they were expected to behave towards the regime. They had mouths only to keep shut, hands only to make obeisance, knees only to bend and kneel, backs only to bend, and bodies only to shrink before the authorities. But they had a difficult time doing all this while trying to keep their goats under control. They had to safeguard their place in the queue as well as protect their animals and possessions. As the sun rose higher and higher, everyone covered their heads with a cloth. There were many different kinds of people around that compound. Poonachi grew frightened and took refuge in the old woman's lap.

'Lie down without butting your head against me. Don't be scared, baby. It will be no worse than being pricked by a thorn.' The old woman stroked Poonachi's body to calm her nerves.

'Why are they piercing the ears of these goats, ayah?' asked a young girl behind her in a secretive whisper.

'So it will be a marker for each goat,' the old woman

replied the way she knew it. 'They will pierce an ear and hang a hoop from it. There is a number embedded in it, they say. With that number, they can find out everything about the goat. Goats have horns, don't they? Suppose they get a little angry and point them at the regime? Such goats have to be identified, right? That's why they all have to get their ears pierced.'

'That's not it, ayah. Our government needs statistics on how many goats there are in this province – how many goats and how many sheep – how many give milk, how many are pregnant, and so on. It's for that purpose,' said a man from the back of the queue.

'Yes. If goats get lost, we'll be able to find them. Even if they are stolen, we can get them back. If a goat gets angry and hides somewhere, we'll know where it is. There's more to it than simply piercing an ear. When it's looked at under sunlight, a glow will emanate from it. People like us can't see it, but it will be visible to the regime,' said another man.

'But goats are so docile. What crime can they possibly commit?' asked the young woman.

'It's not so easy to herd goats and look after them, girl. They are stealthy. If we are not alert, they'll enter a field and destroy the crop. We have to fasten them with a rope when they are grazing, tie their hind legs together with the rope around their necks. If we don't keep a strict watch on them, they'll become arrogant and do anything they want. "We were in the forest once, we'll go back there," they'll say, and run away.'

'Yes, indeed. Not for nothing do they say, "When goats get together, it spells danger."'

'You can say what you want. But when did goats ever come together ... or raise their horns to butt us? They have horns only to scratch themselves, right?' said the man from the back.

'Even so, we have to be careful, don't we?' retorted another. They all agreed and had a hearty laugh.

'That's all very well, but why do they make us stand in the queue under the hot, baking sun?' one of the men interjected.

'We don't have the habit of standing in queues. That's why they are training us.'

'Why should we be trained to stand in queues?'

'The present situation may not last forever, right? When we have to go around looking for food to eat, we shouldn't beat up and kill one another, see? If we get used to queues right now, there won't be any problem in the future, right?'

'Not really, man. A lot of people come to the countryside. They promise jobs and take away everyone who is working in the fields. They exploit such workers to the hilt, then throw them away like waste pulp. What do we do after that? Even if we want a matchstick, it won't be easy to get one. We'll have to stand in a queue. That's why we are being trained.'

'Oh, what a character you are! Go on. Every year the water we get from rainfall keeps going down. If this continues, famine will surely set in. Then the regime itself will open gruel stands and feed everyone. And our people shouldn't fight among themselves and die when that happens, right? That's why we are training ourselves to stand in queues today.'

'We have to get used to queues.'

'We must make queuing a habit.'

'It's important to train ourselves for queues.'

'We need queues for everything.'

'We must get used to standing in queues.'

'We must get used to waiting in queues.'

'Queues will make us patient.'

'Queues will make us tolerant.'

'Must get used to queues.'

'Must make queues a habit.'

'Anyway, only those of us who own just one or two goats have to suffer like this. We drag our goats and kids along in this scorching heat and stand for long hours in the queue. It's such an ordeal. What happens to those who have one or two hundred goats?'

'Haven't you heard? The regime has made arrangements to send its officers to them. They will get the ear-piercing done for their goats, eat their food and come back. It is we who must suffer.'

'I know. There's a man in our village who owns a thousand goats. Just think: a thousand goats! If he opens the yard and lets them out, all the fields and groves will look like goats. And even that's nothing. When they spread out to graze, we'd think the whole world is made up of goats. That's what it would look like. How can the officer who comes to pierce their ears even count the number of goats? Whatever the owner says will become his head count. If you grease his palm with a few coins, he will close his eyes, pierce the ears of only those kids that are pointed out to him, bow and scrape before the owner, and come back.'

'That's the way it is, ayah. When did the rich ever suffer any hardship? It's only poor people who come here like fools to stand in the queue and suffer.'

'Speak softly, sir. The regime has ears on all sides.'

'There's an old saying that the regime is deaf.'

'It's deaf only when we speak about our problems. When we talk about the regime, its ears are quite sharp.'

Their chatter went on for a long time.

6

WHEN THE OFFICERS finally arrived and the piercing of ears was about to begin, shouts rang out that a man at the back of the queue had fainted. An officer came rushing to the spot.

'Wretched dogs. They put nothing in their bellies before they come here early in the morning and stand in the queue. Then they collapse in a faint, holding up our work. It happens all the time. Take him and put him in the shade, give him some water. If anyone faints from now on, tell them their goats won't get their ears pierced today; they will have to come back next week,' the officer instructed his assistants. They carried the man away. It was rumoured that an old man had fainted like this last week and eventually died.

Those standing in the queue took out water, gruel or food from their baskets and poured it down their gullet to quench their hunger. They covered their heads to shield themselves from the sun, the men with their towels and the women using the free end of their saris. Even a brief fainting spell would ruin their chance of getting the job done and they would have to come back again the next week. Policemen turned up every now and then and restored order to the queue using their sticks. 'Stand in the queue, stand in the queue,' was their steady refrain.

The sheep owners had an issue with this process. Each sheep had only one lamb, but goats kept arriving with up to five kids each. Till all the five kids of a goat had got their ears pierced, a sheep owner with a single lamb had to wait. 'Everyone can get only one kid's ear pierced at a time. If the work has to be done for another kid, they have to stand in the queue again,' they insisted. The goat owners opposed this vehemently. 'If you want, make your sheep have a litter of three or four,' they retorted. If the goat owners had to return to the queue every time they had to get a kid's ear pierced, they might have to stand for a whole month. The dispute escalated into fisticuffs. The policemen turned up immediately and tried to mediate. Those who did not obey their instructions received a couple of blows.

An officer came out, stood in front of the crowd and declared in a loud voice: 'All of you must cooperate with the government. It's an individual who stands in the queue. He may have as many kids with him as he likes. There is no law to restrict that number. Unless everyone adjusts to the rules, our work can't proceed smoothly.'

He also announced that the regime was examining a proposal to have a separate queue for goat owners; they should desist from fighting until that came to pass. 'If anybody kicks up a row, I am going to stop work,' he warned the crowd. Even the low murmurs died down immediately and there was complete silence in the compound.

The old woman minded the kids with due vigilance. She had prior experience of being here, several times. It was while standing in the queue that she could meet a few people and chat with them about sundry matters, past and present. Else, she was left to languish alone on a deserted farm with no one for company.

The queue began to move. The old woman let the kids feed at the nanny goat's udder. Poonachi also got two mouthfuls of milk. When she was pregnant, this nanny goat had allowed Poonachi to sleep beside her. After delivering two kids of her own, she wouldn't let Poonachi come anywhere near. Like any other mother goat, she pushed her away. Poonachi could not understand this. Taking the old woman's fingers for teats, she would suck on them. The old woman would offer them to her with a laugh, saying, 'There is honey in my fingers, baby. Suck on them nicely and drink up.'

The old woman grew nervous when it was finally her turn. The assistant examined the ear-piercing done previously for the nanny goat. He tried to read the number embedded in it using a magnifying glass. Nothing was visible. It was all black.

'What's the number of this goat, ayah?' he asked the old woman.

'I don't know about number and all, sami,' she told him.

'You let her graze in all kinds of places. The number gets worn out and erased. You people bring us no end of trouble,' he complained.

'Sami, whatever you inscribe now, please do it in such a way that we can see it clearly,' said the old woman.

'Look at her cheek! Are you saying that what we inscribe is not clear?'

'No, sami. You are the government. Why would I speak a single word against you? You are the one who is in trouble because you can't read the number. That's why I said it,' the old woman explained humbly.

'In whose name is she registered?' The assistant asked her and noted it down. Then he took out a big register, verified the name and read out a number. The officer looked at the register and said, 'When was the last time she had a litter before this one?'

'Last year, sami,' replied the old woman.

'How many kids in that litter?'

'Two.'

'Now?'

'Three, sami.'

'How did it become three this time?'

'It's not in our hands, is it? It's what Mesayyan chooses to give us.'

'Both the male kids are white. This one is black.'

'The males take after the mother; the female after the father.'

'In which village did you mate her with the buck? Whose buck was he? Was he black, too? Do you have his number?' He flung question after question at her.

'So many bucks come to the pasture, sami. How can we tell which one mated with her?' said the old woman.

'I wouldn't know about that. But the next time you come here, you have to give me the number of the buck who has fathered this kid,' said the officer in a stern voice.

They pierced the ears of both the male kids. The kids wailed furiously. The old woman handed over Poonachi as the third. 'What's this? Why have you brought a kitten here? Is it really a goat's kid?' asked the officer.

'It's a female, sami. It was the last in the litter. It's very weak. I am hoping I'll be able to save it somehow,' replied the old woman politely.

'Oho,' said the assistant. He lifted Poonachi and pierced her left earlobe with a thick, long needle, then put a hoop through it. The ear started bleeding. Poonachi cried out in pain.

'Look here, sami. Why not do it gently?' The old woman's tone was a bit harsh.

'Hmm ... the way you're talking is not proper, is it? Oho, this kid doesn't look like it was delivered by that nanny goat. Let's see the mother feed her,' said the officer.

'It *is* the nanny goat's kid, sami. I saw her cry out in pain and talked out of turn, sami. Don't mind it, sami. Please forgive, sami.' The old woman paid obeisance, gathered all her possessions in a hurry and got away quickly, escaping by a whisker.

Poonachi felt as if a boulder was suspended from her left ear. When she tried to flap her ear, drops of blood scattered. Leaving the queue, the old woman went and sat in the shade of a tree. The two male kids had no problem with their ears. Even if they flapped them, there was no bleeding. Their ears had been pierced at the correct spot. In Poonachi's case, the needle had struck a vein in her ear, causing it to bleed. The old woman plucked a leaf from a plant nearby and pressed it on the wound. The bleeding seemed to be under control.

'The poor kid has gone through so much. What a bunch of ruffians they are. They didn't even care that she's a newborn and stabbed her so hard in the ear. May their fingers be deformed by leprosy and wither away,' the old woman cursed.

7

POONACHI CAME DOWN with a fever the same night. Her body was burning up. Her lips were scorched by the heat. Her lashes were gummed together. The blood from the wound had dried and crusted over. When the old woman laid her palm on the kid's body, it was scalding hot. It was normal for goat kids to come down with fever after getting their ears pierced. But she had never encountered such a high fever before.

The old man came over, lifted one of Poonachi's earlobes and looked. Hanging down like leaves with a light curl at the tip, Poonachi's ears made her look beautiful. Examining the earlobe while he stroked it gently, he noticed that the ear-piercing needle had plunged slightly away from the correct spot. It had damaged a nerve. So, that explained the high fever. If a goat owner caused even the slightest problem, the man in charge of piercing showed off his intelligence in this way. Some kids even died from the brute force of his stab. For others, it was a long time before the wound healed eventually.

'Di, you wretched old thing, did you pick a quarrel with

that dog? See how he has punctured a nerve! Why don't you stay out of trouble?' the old man yelled at her. She rushed over to Poonachi and looked at the kid's earlobe. Pus dripped continuously from the wound. The kid had slumped weakly to the ground.

'I said nothing at all. I just asked him to be careful with the needle,' the old woman said.

'Folks like us can survive only if we hold our tongue. Even when they hit us on the back, we should only mumble to ourselves. We shouldn't even breathe if our neighbours can hear us. You've survived all these years, yet you don't know even this much.'

'If you knew everything, you could have taken the kid there, couldn't you? You were scared and hid yourself, and now you have the nerve to talk?'

They argued for a long time, neither conceding to the other. While they talked, the old woman brought different kinds of leaves and squeezed the juice on Poonachi's wound. Whenever she felt a burning sensation, Poonachi raised her head slightly and cried out. The old woman brought warm water and gave it to Poonachi through the tip of an earthen lamp, as if feeding a baby. She thought Poonachi's time would be up soon, but she couldn't give up on her, could she? She also believed that Poonachi couldn't die since she had taken a vow of supplication to Mesayyan, her god.

The kid did manage to survive. But the wound refused to heal quickly. It festered and bled. The old woman kept trying different cures using sundry leaves and herbs. The wound filled with pus and dripped constantly. If she even touched Poonachi's ear, the kid cried out in agony. The old woman had never heard a more plaintive cry. It gave her the shivers. She squeezed the pus out, washed the wound with lukewarm water and bandaged it with leaves. It became one of her daily tasks.

'If some dog passing by on the trail gives him something, should he take it and bring it home? Why couldn't he keep his wits about him? Now he has dumped her on me and gone off to sleep in the fields.' Even as she cursed her husband, the old woman did everything she could to take care of Poonachi.

The pus dried up only after a month. Slowly, the wound scabbed over. During that entire month, Poonachi never left the old woman's side. She would follow the woman while she cooked and swept the house. When she was eating, Poonachi stood next to her.

'This is not for you. I'll give you something else,' the old woman would say affectionately. True to her word, she would drain the water in which oilcake had been soaked overnight, warm it up slightly, pour it into a bottle and feed Poonachi through the attached tube.

Poonachi liked the taste of oilcake water. Taking the old woman's hand for a mother goat's udder, she bumped against it as she drank. 'It will flow even without your bumping, kannu. Drink up,' the old woman would say.

8

FOR THE OLD woman, raising Poonachi was like looking after a baby in her old age. The void in her home in the wake of her daughter's departure after marriage was being filled by the kid. These days she hardly quarrelled with the old man. She served him food with love. The old man, too, spoke a couple of sweet words to her while eating. At night, Poonachi slept beside the old woman on her cot. She learnt to jump off the bed and go outside the shed whenever she wanted to pee or shit. 'The kid is so disciplined!' the old woman marvelled each time.

When the goats that went out daily for grazing returned home at dusk, Poonachi would go up to them. Kalli's three kids had grown quite big now. They were tethered at night, and scarcely took notice of Poonachi. Even if she went near them, they blessed her with their snouts and sent her away. Semmi's two kids, however, would always come running to play with Poonachi. Both were bucks. One would butt Poonachi in the face; the other would butt her from behind. Poonachi would crouch, put her head down and scoot away.

Without Poonachi in the middle, the two heads would bang into each other. The bucks did their best to avoid this, and Poonachi would pull back at the right moment to make it happen – this was a favourite game for all three. Once in a rare while, Poonachi would win. On those days, she would spill over with joy. She would run straight to the old woman and rub her face against her shins. 'Such a gloater she is!' the old woman would laugh.

Now and again, Poonachi would get to suckle a few mouthfuls of milk from Semmi. After starting Poonachi on oilcake water, the old woman didn't bother much about feeding her milk. If there was something left over from the milk she drew from Kalli for the old man, she would pour it in a bottle and give it to Poonachi. While suckling her kids, Semmi would stand still, as though lost in a trance, head tilted upward and eyes closed, her mouth working away. At such times, Poonachi would try to compete with Semmi's kids. Trying to suckle too fast, they would lose hold of a teat. Poonachi would sneak in during that interval and grab one. She would get to drink a couple of mouthfuls of the delicious nectar. Meanwhile, the kid who had let go of the teat would push Poonachi aside and grab it back. In this way, Poonachi learnt to feed by stealth.

Even so, her health did not improve. She still looked like a malnourished baby. Her body had gained a little weight, but the hair on her skin hung in matted strands. Her swollen belly stuck out like a fist. Her eyes were pallid and lifeless. She moved about with difficulty. However, as her ear wound dried up, she regained some strength and vitality. Slowly she began to nibble at blades of grass, one at a time. The old woman got her used to it. She plucked tender leaves from a gulmohur tree and fed them to Poonachi. The bitter taste didn't agree with the kid's palate. But the old woman didn't give up. She pushed the leaves gently between Poonachi's teeth. Once she started chewing, she learned to like the taste. In the same way, the old woman got her used to different types of leaves and grass as well. Kiluva leaves and scotch grass were Poonachi's favourites. Whenever they were available, she ate heartily. This was how Poonachi passed the first two months of her life.

Around the beginning of the third month, she went out to graze with the other goats. Driving the goats to the pasture and grazing them was the old man's job. As soon as dawn broke, he would sweep and clean the floor of the cattle shed. It wasn't a huge area: the droppings of two goats and five or six kids, along with two big lumps of dung from a lone buffalo calf were all he had to deal with. There was just enough to fill a couple of baskets. He would gather the whole lot and dump it in the compost pit. Then he would lay out some dry stalks or a little grass for the buffalo calf, who would eagerly devour the feed. Expecting that they would also get something to eat, the goats would cry at him.

Whenever the old woman went to work in other people's fields, she brought home some unripe babul fruit, thistle leaves and hariyali grass, which she stored carefully. Her husband would put some of it in a basket and keep it at the centre of the hut where the goats were tethered. Five or six heads would butt the basket. The lucky ones managed to get something.

Poonachi kept away from the fracas. Since she wasn't tied up like the other goats, she was free to move around. She could go and eat whatever she fancied, whenever she wanted. The old woman didn't object. This puny kid was not going to eat up very much, was she? If Poonachi stood next to her while she was eating, she would give the kid a fistful of her own food. If, on a rare day, there was cooked rice, Poonachi devoured it with relish. If not, she would pick at the curry leaves and discarded chilli skins and come away. To prevent her from putting her mouth into their food, the old woman kept every pot in the house tightly covered with a cloth.

After laying out the feed for the goats, the old man would tighten his loincloth and set out for the fields. No one knew where he went or what he did, but he always came back with a foot-long neem twig stuck in his mouth. He would keep chewing on it even after coming home. Finally he would rinse his mouth, wash his face and sit down to eat. The goats that had been awaiting his arrival would keep looking at him once he was home. Wherever he happened to go, their heads would turn in that direction. Now and again, a cry would be heard. Kalli's kids were in robust health, and they would tug at their rope and bleat in excitement. The old man scarcely paid them any attention. It was the old woman who would shout at them to keep quiet.

In the morning, the old man ate only mashed rice. As he pulped the rice, Poonachi would sidle up to him. The old man would then be reminded of his own childhood. He would pretend to be oblivious to Poonachi's presence. After waiting for some time, the kid would position herself directly in front of him. Still he would not look at her. She would bite his hand. He would snatch it free. She would try to put her snout in the rice pot. He would raise his hand as if to hit her, then bring it down slowly and pat her on the mouth. Poonachi would pretend to writhe in pain and raise a plaintive cry. The old woman was sure to hear it. While carrying on with her work, she would say, 'Yov, the poor kid is crying. Why can't you give her a little? If you eat with a hungry kid watching, you will die of stomach ache.'

He would immediately take a small bit of the raw onion that accompanied the rice and hold it out to Poonachi. She would take it in her wide open mouth and run to the hut, then stand in front of the other goats and chew the onion. Poonachi loved the pungent taste of onion caressing her tongue. Even after she had eaten the bit, she would continue chewing with nothing in her mouth. The nanny goats and their kids would stare at her with a glint of envy in their eyes. Poonachi would then perform a leap. In that leap was the boastful question: 'Do you all know the taste of an onion?'

After drinking up the rice gruel, the old man would sit in the shade and smoke a cheroot. It looked as if he had broken off a goat's leg and stuck it between his lips. If Poonachi rubbed against his shin when he was enjoying a smoke, he would kick out furiously. So she stopped going anywhere near him then.

Each time he finished smoking, the old woman would bring a basket outside. The basket held his lunch as well as a weeding hook. He would free the goats and then bind each goat's neck to its forelegs with the rope in order to restrict their movement. Then he would wait till the kids had finished suckling. The kids were not yet bound with ropes. They were still not used to walking past their mother. When they left the front yard after drinking up all the water in the trough, the old man would put the basket on his head and follow them.

Poonachi would look on wistfully as the herd of goats set out for grazing. It would be dusk by the time they returned. Until then, she would have to keep weaving in and out between the old woman's legs. It was very hard on her.

One day, when she was looking on dejectedly, the old man said: 'Get Poonachi to hurry up. Let her start grazing with the goats.' His wife wouldn't agree. 'Can she walk that far?' 'Could a wildcat carry her away?' 'Will she last till you come down after sunset?' She had a lot of questions.

The old man shook with laughter. 'Come here, di, Poonachi.' When he stretched out his hand and called her, she ran to him. He lifted her into his arms, placed her across his shoulder and started walking. With her legs hanging on

54

either side of his shoulder, Poonachi raised her head and cried out to the old woman. The old woman couldn't tell if it was a cry of sorrow or joy.

'I'll be back,' Poonachi said, as she happily took her leave.

9

FROM HER PERCH atop the old man's shoulder, Poonachi felt like she was floating on air. She cast a friendly glance at the weaver birds flying overhead. By then she had acquired the majestic bearing of a king riding his royal chariot. But it didn't last very long. The old man, who was holding her legs on one side with a slight downward tug, put her on the ground after they had gone some distance. 'Run along now. Graze with the other goats,' he said, chasing her away.

They were on the same hillock where he had received Poonachi from Bakasuran. She ran off to frolic with her fellow creatures. The hillock was quite small, like a pile of sand that children like to play with, but it hosted a cluster of hill mango, babul, black sirissa and palai trees. Their trunks were wholly covered by a tangle of creepers. There were thickets of glory bower and veldt grape as well. The deep trench adjoining the field extended far into the distance.

When they reached the field, they found that a large flock of sheep was already grazing there. Some goatherds were moving about. There were very few goats, though. The old man grazed his goats on the hillock itself because there was nothing for them to graze on level ground. Despite the rope restricting her movements, Kalli stood with her forelegs planted precariously on the tree trunks, pulling their branches downward with her snout and grazing on the leaves. Once she pulled down a branch, her kids along with Semmi ran over and caught hold of it. They held the branch down together and ate all the leaves on it. When they were done eating, they would release the branch abruptly. Like a bow whose string had snapped, the branch swung upward again.

For Poonachi, the environment and the grazing were new and strange. She floundered, not knowing what to do. She ran behind the other goats. She was so tiny that all she could see were legs. Since she was unable to push herself between the legs, she couldn't eat a single leaf. She was afraid she might be knocked down. She continued to stare at the goats for some time. Then she picked and ate the scraps of leaves that they had scattered on the ground while eating. After the first frenzied rush, once their hunger was quenched, the goats calmed down. Then individually or in small groups, they dispersed and started grazing.

Poonachi was relieved. Since the hillock was full of her favourite hill mango trees, she walked towards them. From a branch that was bent under the unbearable weight of creepers, she ate as much as she wanted. Eating like this made her happy. Planting her hooves on the dirt mound and climbing up and down filled her with joy. Kalli's three kids – Kaduvayan, Peethan and Porumi – didn't bother at all about Poonachi. Their world happened to be different from hers. Kaduvayan alone came near her now and then, sniffed her vagina, pressed his mouth on it and raised his head. Savouring the thrill with his snout pointed upward, he lifted a hind leg and tried to rest it on her.

Poonachi was frightened. Firmly covering her vagina with her tail, she ran away from the spot. She could sense him staring at her now and again as if he wanted to tell her, 'Just you wait. Do you think you will get away from me?'

Peethan had many friends there, and was busy roaming around with them. But the next time Kaduvayan came near Poonachi, Porumi rushed up and butted him with her bare head, then pushed him away. She pressed her snout on Poonachi's belly, indicating that she should go further away.

Oothan and Uzhumban were Semmi's kids. Both bucks were younger than Poonachi. She was happy to play and run around with them.

Climbing the small boulder on the hillock and jumping down from there seemed to be their favourite game. So Poonachi climbed the boulder and stood on it too. It had a rough surface, but it sloped down steeply, ending in a sharp point. As she walked gingerly towards the point, her whole body slid downward. Her intestines rose to her throat. Standing with her forelegs firmly planted, she relaxed her hindquarters till she felt light as cotton, then she sprang forward. She landed right below the sharp point with her hooves steady on the ground. Her legs were trembling. Oothan and Uzhumban kept climbing and jumping off, one following the other. She had proved herself by jumping once. I don't want to do this anymore, thought Poonachi. But if she left the game after a single jump, they would look down on her. She climbed on top of the boulder once again.

Though her legs were trembling, she flexed her body and brought the tremors under control. Then she jumped once more. By now she was confident that she could jump a few more times. But there was no strength left in her body. The other two kids were suckled by their mother. Their bodies were bursting with energy. Rice water and oilcake served to keep Poonachi alive, but gave her little strength. She was gasping for breath and her legs were tired. She acted as if she no longer had any interest in the game and moved away. She tugged at a scarlet gourd creeper and bit into it. Its leaves had a really good taste. She was eager to sample all the varieties of leaves and foliage to be found in the area. However, after eating some leaves from the creeper, she felt like lying down. She walked over to the black sirissa tree and rested in its shade.

After having stayed for so long in the old woman's house under the protection of a roof, her body was not used to the rigours of wandering around in the hot sun across fields and hilly terrain. But she liked it. From now on, she would come here every day.

As she lay there, she saw Oothan and Uzhumban playing a game. Trying to show off before her, both bucks leapt and jumped over and over again. While performing one such leap, Oothan twisted his neck, fell flat on the ground and cried out in pain. Hearing the sound, the old man came running. He couldn't make out what had happened. He thought that the two kids must have butted heads and fought with each other. 'I'll skin your hides,' he yelled at them. Oothan, who had recovered by then, got up, walked slowly over to Poonachi and lay down beside her. Fearing that he was badly hurt, she tried to lick his body and offer him solace.

All Poonachi had to do in the pasture was to run around busily, eat some leaves and fill her belly. She could jump and play, lie down in the shade and go to sleep. She also came in contact with a flock of sheep that came to graze there. But she took a strong dislike to the lambs. They always had their heads down. One must bow one's head while grazing or drinking water, she reflected. Why did these lambs keep their heads down even while walking? Can you call it living when you live without looking at anything but the ground? The trees, the moon, the stars, daylight – had these lambs ever looked at any of those marvels? Unless we look up, how can we see the sky? They even sniffled, cleared their throats and sneezed while looking at the ground. They didn't see the faces in front of them. They only looked at the legs of the other sheep and stood with their heads wedged between those legs. Even when she wanted to play with a lamb, it came running with its head down!

Look at the goats now, Poonachi said to herself. They always stood with their heads held high. They focussed only on the leaves that they could eat with their heads up. While walking, they looked straight ahead. When the goatherd called, they followed him with their heads held high.

None of the sheep had their neck and forelegs bound together with a rope. That was only done to the proud goats, who were forced to look at the ground as they walked. Goats always tried to break free of their shackles. Sheep had none, so they didn't need to make the effort. If it was in your nature to bow down, why would anyone shackle you? And yet, they were fortunate, these sheep. They had no inkling that to bow was to be shackled.

10

OOOTHAN AND UZHUMBAN were Poonachi's only playmates. Her days passed in fighting as well as getting along with them. A couple of memorable incidents took place during that period, when they roamed carefree in the pasture. Both involved Kaduvayan and Peethan. As soon as he entered the pasture, Kaduvayan would get all fired up. With his head thrown back, he would survey the field. He would look for places where goats' heads were visible and run towards them. 'Dei, Kaduvaya ... I'll break your legs!' the old man would shout. Kaduvayan would have turned stone deaf by then.

He would visit every herd in the pasture and sniff the vaginas of the mother goats as well as the female kids. Then, with his upper lip pushed back to bare his teeth and head held high, he would relish the smell. He would stick out his penis and piss noisily. Entranced by his touch, a couple of female kids would contract their bodies and start peeing. Kaduvayan would put his snout in the stream of piss and drink a little. A few mother goats would butt him and knock him down. The female kids would become frightened and run away, their tails firmly in place.

Poonachi observed Kaduvayan's antics and grew to hate him. The old man was no good; had his wife been around, she would have given Kaduvayan a couple of blows on his snout and set him right, Poonachi thought.

Kaduvayan would wander about for a long time and amble back, exhausted, to his own herd. Then he would graze properly. When no one was looking, he would chase Poonachi. She would run crying to the old man. 'So you won't leave even a little baby alone? That's how cheeky you've become!' the old man would scold and chase him away. He would lift Poonachi on to his lap, keep her there for some time and then send her off to graze.

Poonachi had no trouble with Peethan. He didn't go rushing anywhere. His sole target was Porumi, who was always close at hand. He was constantly up to mischief with her, caressing her or trying to put his legs on her. Sometimes Porumi enjoyed his attention. At other times, she would turn her face away. If the old man was around, he would give Peethan a hard kick. 'So, you want to lie around here drinking your sister's piss. Call yourself a buck, you lazy slob?' the old man would scold him. Whenever they mingled with other herds, Peethan would chase after a few female kids. He never went looking for them on his own.

Other goatherds would complain to the old man about Kaduvayan's behaviour. 'Thatha, we are fed up of your kid's mischief. When our goats are grazing, he licks them all over and chases after them. Just get him fixed.'

'Let him be, poor thing. He is also a living creature. Let him fuck at least one doe. Then we can castrate him,' the old man would say.

'If he fucks a doe, he'll lose control.'

'Let him taste that pleasure at least once in this life. Just the memory will be enough for him,' the old man laughed.

Kaduvayan couldn't be controlled. He continued to chase after female goats and disrupt their grazing. When the complaints about him mounted, the old man bound him tight. There was no gap at all between the kid's head and forelegs. Kaduvayan could not bear it. He shook his head violently and tried to lift his forelegs high, but he couldn't undo the rope. Once or twice, he jumped up high and fell down. Then he learnt to bend one foreleg, lift it off the ground and hobble around on three legs. With a crippled leg, he tried to chase female goats. But his unruly behaviour had been largely tamed. No rope was tied around Peethan's legs. He indulged in his pranks quietly and escaped punishment.

One day, from another herd that came to the pasture, an inviting scent wafted across the field and greatly unsettled Kaduvayan. He tried to head there with the shackle around his legs. The old man could not smell the scent. He stopped Kaduvayan. But Kaduvayan would not calm down. He refused to graze even a mouthful. He kept crying out in the direction of the scent. In answer, a cry rang out from there too.

Then the man in charge of the herd came to the old man with a proposal: 'One of my does is in heat. It's been writhing and calling since last night. Shall we try setting your buck on her?'

The old man was overjoyed. Immediately, he untied the rope around Kaduvayan's forelegs.

In one leap, Kaduvayan crossed over to the writhing doe. And there he stayed the whole day. His form, standing beside her, placing both forelegs on her body now and again, was visible to Poonachi like a distant shadow. She couldn't understand what he was doing. Nor was it clear to her why the old man or the goatherd didn't chase him away. They kept glancing at Kaduvayan once in a while, talking and laughing.

Poonachi didn't like it at all. If the old woman came to know about it, her husband would be done for, she imagined. Every night Poonachi told the old woman everything that had happened that day in the pasture. Of what she recounted, the old woman would understand some things and not others. Nevertheless, she was always a keen listener. 'See how much this kid knows!' she would say, cradling Poonachi's face in her hands and planting a kiss on it. Poonachi decided that she must tell the old woman that very night about this horrible incident.

Peethan walked over to where Kaduvayan stood. He went to the doe and rubbed against her. Kaduvayan would not let him get close. With a single head butt, he sent Peethan away, crying in pain. In the afternoon, the old man tied the rope around Kaduvayan's neck and forelegs again. Dejected, Kaduvayan lay down in the shade. He didn't eat even a mouthful the whole day.

Now Peethan wandered after the doe. Perhaps because she didn't like him, the doe kept running away. Peethan didn't give up, though. He ran after her. It appeared as if the doe consented and stood still sometimes out of pity for him. A short while later, Peethan came back and started grazing.

The old man undid the rope from around Kaduvayan's neck and forelegs. He went directly to the doe and stood before her.

'See how different every living creature is from the others,' the old man said.

'The kid is done with her lust. Now she won't let any buck come near her,' the goatherd remarked, laughing.

But Kaduvayan didn't come back to his herd the whole day. At dusk, when it was time to drive the goats back, the old man caught hold of him and brought him back. The doe turned in their direction and bleated. Kaduvayan called out in response. The sorrow that rang through both voices struck Poonachi as very strange.

'I feel sorry for them. Why don't you let him stay back just for today? Let him spend the night with her and come back,' the goatherd said.

'Take him with you by all means. I'll arrange for someone to castrate him tomorrow morning. Let him enjoy himself for a night,' the old man said, giving his assent.

Once he was released, Kaduvayan entered the herd and

stood rubbing himself against the doe's body. He never turned to look at his own herd again. His mother cried out to him. He didn't look back. Peethan cried. He didn't respond. Porumi cried out. He didn't look back for her sake, either. Seeing someone who belonged with them going away, Poonachi too gave a feeble cry. He never turned. The doe's call outweighed all their cries.

'When it's time to mate, who has the time for other affections?' said the old man, exhaling a deep sigh.

The old woman chided her husband for leaving Kaduvayan with a different herd. 'Why, all you had to do was to bring that doe here. Why should our buck stay over there? What improper custom is this!' she said.

'Look, it's only for today. If that doe had come here, would she not have been scared in a new place? Kaduvayan is hardly aware of anything apart from her. That's why I thought they would be happy over there and left him behind,' the old man said, trying to appease her.

'Is she such a vamp that he had to go behind her?' the old woman said.

'Vamp or not, she has a pretty nose. He has fallen for her. Moreover, she is the first one he has been with. Even if he wants to leave her, do you think his body will let him?' the old man said, laughing.

'He won't even remember our house anymore. Call that man first thing tomorrow morning and castrate Kaduvayan. That'll make him stay put in one place,' the old woman said.

That night the old man and his wife talked endlessly

about the problem of Kaduvayan. When they woke up, they talked some more. These days, Poonachi slept either under the old woman's cot or next to the goats in their hut. She would go to the spot where Oothan and Uzhumban slept with their heads pointing in opposite directions, and lie down between them. Semmi didn't like her intruding in this manner. Tugging at her tether, she would try to butt Poonachi, but the kid was out of her reach. Poonachi would lie still and relish Semmi's predicament. Semmi would fly into a rage, but what could she do? Once, she pointed her behind in Poonachi's direction, crouched and started to pee. Poonachi was anointed with a shower of piss. 'Chee.' She got up and fled in horror and disgust. Whenever she recalled how the same Semmi had lovingly protected her before Oothan and Uzhumban were born, she would start weeping. She had thought of Semmi as her own mother. Now Semmi kept showing Poonachi every day that she was not.

Kalli cried all through that night. Already pregnant with her next litter, she had no milk to give these days. Nevertheless, she kept her three kids constantly under her protective care. She would look at Peethan and Porumi and cry, as if to ask: 'Where is Kaduvayan?' They would bleat back at her in response.

Kaduvayan's absence might well have pleased Peethan. Kaduvayan was a champion at drawing attention to himself. Peethan was happy to lie around, chewing the cud. 'I am the only one for you, always,' he informed his mother.

Though Kaduvayan had gone away with a different herd,

the night seemed a very happy one to Poonachi. But all that happiness went up in smoke the next day.

Well before they reached the pasture, Kaduvayan had already arrived. He took scarcely any notice of his former playmates. It didn't seem as if any food had gone into his belly either. Had he at least drunk some water? He followed Pretty Nose everywhere, and she led him on nicely. Today she had firmly covered her vagina with her thick tail. Kaduvayan got behind her and tried to push the tail away with his snout, but she wouldn't give in to his desire. He did not budge from her side, constantly hovering around her. The moment she lifted her tail, he leapt forward and mounted her. She did not resist. It made Poonachi angry. Why did this Pretty Nose stand there passively? Why should she bear the weight of Kaduvayan's huge body?

The old man saw them too. 'All right. This is the last time, as you'll see,' he laughed.

11

WITHIN A FEW minutes, a man had turned up from somewhere. He was nearly the same age as the old man and much taller than him. He carried a pair of wooden scissor sticks as well as a big water-gourd shell.

'Come, boatman. It's well past sunrise. I was wondering why there was no sign of you yet.'

Meanwhile, four or five goatherds had also come over. 'I had to finish my previous job before coming here, didn't I?' said the boatman as he placed the water-gourd shell on the ground. The men extended their bowls to him, and he poured some toddy for each of them from the shell. Curious to find out what was happening, Poonachi walked over to them.

'Why does this kid look like a baby donkey with matted hair?' said the boatman.

'We are raising her on our own. Any kid who doesn't have her parents' attention is bound to be shabby,' replied the old man. Poonachi rushed to hide behind him.

'All right. Catch the kid and bring him here,' said the boatman. 'Bu-ku-koo, bu-ku-koo,' the old man tried calling

Kaduvayan. It didn't seem as though Kaduvayan heard his call. Two young goatherds began to walk in measured steps towards him. Pretty Nose became frightened on seeing them approach. Thinking that she was the one in danger, Kaduvayan bristled, raised his head and charged towards them. 'Ah, he is going to protect her, it seems,' laughed one of the goatherds as he stepped forward and planted himself in front of Kaduvayan.

Another man, who was following behind, reached out and caught hold of one of Kaduvayan's hind legs and lifted it up. Unable to stand on three legs, Kaduvayan stumbled and fell sideways on the ground. 'A big dick but a dented belly,' laughed the man in front of him. The next moment, Kudavayan found himself being pulled along by the rope around his neck. He had no option but to follow them. He looked back often and kept bleating so that Pretty Nose could hear him. Too stunned to think of responding to his call, she stood stock still for a few moments. Then she came running after him, crying pitifully. It's a miracle that there's a creature who cries so earnestly for this Kaduvayan, thought Poonachi.

The goatherd ran towards Pretty Nose and chased her away. She joined the herd and merged with it, turning back occasionally to look at Kaduvayan,

They took Kaduvayan and laid him in front of the boatman. One man held down his head and forelegs. Another held his hind legs pressed to the ground. But Kaduvayan lifted his torso and leapt up.

'He looks like a kid who is mad after meat,' said the boatman.

'He pounced on a female just yesterday. We can't control him anymore. That's why I sent for you,' said the old man.

The boatman went up to Kaduvayan and pulled out his testicles from between his hind legs. The youth who was holding the hind legs up laughed. Opening out the scissor sticks, the boatman placed the testicles between the two arms and pressed down. Something snapped with a loud crack. 'Beyyyyaaaa!' Kaduvayan let out a single long cry. The goats in the pasture stopped grazing and looked up. Even the sheep raised their heads and looked back with their ears stiffening. Everything was over in barely a moment. With tears pouring from his eyes, Kaduvayan collapsed to the ground. Now there was no need for anyone to hold him down.

'All that wild behaviour can go on only while these are intact,' said a youth.

'How will I ever be at peace after doing such terrible things?' rued the boatman.

'Men who slit other people's throats are living without a care. Why do you worry so much?' asked the old man.

By then, they had captured and brought Peethan. The boatman put the water-gourd shell to his lips and drank a little. 'My sin is bigger than the sin of homicide,' he said. Soon the fields resounded with Peethan's heart-rending cry. Next, three rams were brought one after another. The boatman did his work like a seasoned expert. By now the fields had grown used to the cries. Nobody even looked up. The goatherds lifted the male kids who had fallen on the ground and made them stand up. Unable to join his legs together, Kaduvayan kept them splayed wide. His testicles had swollen up. He cried fitfully till he wore himself out. All the male kids did the same. Peethan couldn't even cry. His body was still shaking. None of them was quite aware of what had happened to them.

The boatman drank up all the toddy left in the water-gourd shell. When he looked up, his eyes fell on the five kids standing there in agony, tears streaming from their eyes. He slapped his chest with both hands and burst out crying. 'Sinner! I am a sinner and a wretch!'

The old man walked over to the boatman and scolded him: 'What's the matter? You're not new to the job, are you?' He poured a measure of grain into a towel. The owners of the other kids added their share of grain. The boatman paid no attention. He wailed and wept aloud, slapping the ground and his chest by turns. Kneeling before the row of kids standing in front of him like gods, he paid obeisance to them with folded hands. A stream of gibberish issued from his mouth, as if he were pleading abjectly with them. Then he stood up like a man unhinged and walked back the way he had come. One of the young men ran after him with the bundle of grain. With the bundle swaying back and forth over his shoulder like a large abscess, he walked away in silence.

That night the old man spoke scarcely a word to his

wife. The old woman tried everything she could to make him talk.

'So, you suddenly choose to turn into a dumb owl. On the days you are all smiles and eager to talk, I have to speak to you. When you become mute, I should also shut my mouth,' she said accusingly.

Poonachi was sad that day. Kaduvayan and Peethan did not fold their legs and lie down for even a minute. They stood in the same position all night. Every now and then, they would whimper or cry out suddenly. Poonachi went near Kaduvayan and sniffed his legs. There was no response from him.

The old man had had a difficult time herding them from the pasture to the house that evening. Just putting one foot forward was enough to make them cry out in pain. They kept crying by turns as they walked home. The old man, for his part, drove them patiently. The mother goats were also weary. Kalli, the female goat, went near Kaduvayan and sniffed him as if in greeting. He was in no position to respond.

It seemed as though a profound silence had engulfed them from all sides. Poonachi didn't sleep a wink that night. Every now and then she would go and stand near them for a brief while. They stood immobile, however, like a pair of stone figurines.

At dawn the next day, the old woman fetched water in a big, wide-mouthed vessel she called a kundaan and splashed mugs of water on Kaduvayan and Peethaan's groin with great force. They jerked back in fear and then stood passively. The touch of water on their wounds must have been soothing. The old woman splashed two or three kundaans of water on the kids' wounds. Then she brought some cattle dung and smeared it on their testicles.

'Why chase after those female kids and go through all this trouble? You couldn't keep quiet, it seems. And even if you wanted to, the blood coursing through your veins wouldn't have let you. So now you have no choice but to suffer,' the old woman said to no one in particular as she treated their wounds. She offered the kids some cotton seed from her hand. Kaduvayan wouldn't even sniff them. The old woman didn't give up. She opened his mouth and pushed some inside. As he chewed on them slowly, the taste came through and Kaduvayan ended up munching on some more. Neither of the kids came to the pasture for the next four days. They kept standing in the goat hut all day. Poonachi felt dejected. The whole pasture seemed to be deserted. She lay in the shade, trying to figure out why it had come to this. She couldn't think of anything.

When the herd went home after grazing on the fifth day, both Kaduvayan and Peethan were lying down and chomping on some leaves. On seeing Poonachi and the others, they emitted gentle cries. Poonachi felt cheerful again. The kids came with the others for grazing from the next day onwards. Poonachi ran to Kaduvayan and tried to play with him by dashing and colliding against him. He didn't do anything to her. Nor did he ever go chasing after the female kids in other herds. He kept to himself and the grass he was eating. Just like Peethan, who had always been like that. Now he was even more subdued. Poonachi's eyes drifted occasionally to the space between their legs. She saw the testicles which had once hung there like big palm fruit gradually shrivel, shrink and wither away. Nevertheless, Poonachi was happy that they were subdued and well behaved, and no longer writhing in pain.

12

THE FOLLOWING MONTH, Poonachi went on a pilgrimage and learnt about the outside world for the first time. Until then, the old couple's thatched shed, the field around it, the village and the pasture had been her whole world. The journey made her understand that the world was much bigger. The old woman's daughter had come to take her mother for the annual festival at the Mesagaran temple in her village. The couple followed the custom of taking their goats with them when they went to the festival every year. Before they set out for their daughter's village, the old man took the buffalo calf to the market fair and sold it. They were happy that they had some money to give to their daughter.

They set out after daybreak, with a large container of food for the journey. Poonachi had initially thought that they were headed towards a new pasture. But they kept walking. On that first day, they grazed beside a lake and went to sleep on a set of boulders nearby. They had to identify a spot to halt for the night while there was still daylight. Since their eyes had grown dim with age, they were used to going to bed before nightfall. The wind carried the coolness of the water in the lake and spread it on the boulders. They slept blissfully.

The next day they entered a plantation of palm trees, and walked through it all day. An endless sequence of palm trees, row upon row. The rustle of palm fronds in the breeze. Dried up palm fruit. It was a big sandy plain. The goats filled their bellies by chewing the leaves on the palm stalks and gorging on creepers that the old man pulled down towards them. They had never seen creepers like these in the pasture. Some were very tasty.

Each time the goats ran off in different directions, it was a task for the couple to gather them in one place again and drive them forward. But Poonachi never left the old woman's side. As they walked, she would sometimes trip and fall between the old woman's legs. Even then the old woman did not scold her.

'Poonachi kannu, watch your step. If you crash into my legs and knock me down, who will take care of you? When you have a litter of seven someday, won't you need someone to look after you?' she said affectionately. Poonachi felt terribly shy.

Oothan and Uzhumban gave the couple a lot of trouble. We should have brought them with a rope around their necks, the old woman said. Just carrying the bundle of food was taxing for her. They hurried on, anxious to reach their daughter's village before they ran out of food, or it got spoilt. By their reckoning, they would reach their destination by the evening of the fourth day. At noon on the third day, they reached a wooded hillside. It was a long hill range. A forest filled with tall trees sprawled across the range. They let the goats graze in the foothills. If they walked in a circle along the edge of the forest, they would come to a trail going east by the time they were halfway around. It was a short-cut to the village.

After grazing, the goats drank water from a pond nearby and lay down to rest in the shade. The old man and his wife stretched out for a brief while under a tree. Poonachi lay near the old woman's feet, chewing the cud.

Just then, Oothan and Uzhumban left their mother's side and ran away into the forest. They wanted to play without any interference. Poonachi, who was just waking up, saw them fleeing. Immediately she felt an urge to do the same. She ran behind them. Every tree here had a trunk so big that if five or six men wrapped their arms around it together, it still wouldn't be contained in their embrace. If someone were to hide behind one of these trees, it wouldn't be easy to find him. Oothan tried, but Uzhumban charged around furiously and found him. Poonachi joined the game. Both of them wanted to make Poonachi 'it'. She accepted their decision and played 'it' in the first two rounds.

Both Uzhumban and Oothan ran off and hid. She found Uzhumban by his tail which was sticking out from behind the cover of a tree. But Uzhumban wouldn't concede defeat. She had to come face to face to find him; approaching from the back didn't count because it wasn't fair, Uzhumban argued. Oothan backed him up. Unable to put up with their cheating, Poonachi said, 'To hell with you and your game!' and climbed a little higher. Unripe pods lay strewn on the ground under some trees. She tried biting into a couple of them. They tasted really good. So she wandered further, picking up pods at every tree and eating them along the way.

The forest and the trees seemed miraculous to Poonachi. She saw hare, field rats and snakes that ran away petrified on noticing her. Though afraid, she was also curious. It was a strange feeling, as though she had arrived in her real home. She walked up to a few trees and rubbed her body against a trunk. Only when darkness began to spread slowly among the trees did she wonder if she had walked too far. At once, she began to climb down. But she had lost sight of the track she had made on the way up. In spite of running in several directions and looking all over, she could not find the right way back. She tried crying out. She thought she would hear the old woman's voice raised in answer to her call. But all she heard was the chatter of unfamiliar birds. After a brief while, she fell silent.

Poonachi understood the extent of her intelligence on that day. Darkness fell and all the routes were closed. Left with no other option, she had to spend the night on the hill. Where could she stay? Could she lie down alone, surrounded by the darkness? She was scared. Just then she saw a big pond close by. Water hyacinth covered its whole expanse. She had never before drunk water that tasted so sweet. She wanted to get into the water and swim for a while. But the hyacinth covering the still water made her afraid. She suppressed her wish. Like a hand extending from the edge of the pond, she saw a rock protruding over the water. Wide at the bottom, it became progressively narrow and ended in a sharp point at the top. It looked like the right spot for her. Planting her hooves on the rock, she climbed to the top. No one could get up there. It gave her a sense of security.

At first, Poonachi was consumed by fear. The wind lashed against the trees and ran howling through the forest. Sometimes the trees stood utterly still. She had never before seen the kind of dense, pitch-black darkness that gathered over the pond. She lay clinging to the ground like a rock lizard. After a long while, the moon appeared in the sky, directly overhead, and illuminated the watery expanse of the pond. The forest seemed to come alive suddenly. A few birds rose in the moonlight and flew away. A short while later, a large pack of animals came roaring to the pond, across from the slanted rock on which Poonachi lay. The wild boars looked like silhouettes. They entered the pond, shattering the silence, drinking the water and swimming around in it. Stuck to the rock, Poonachi watched the spectacle. Her eyes welled up for some reason, and she sighed. Her heart was hopelessly eager to jump into the pond, to swim in it and enjoy herself. She knew, however, that she was destined to remain an onlooker. She consoled herself that it was her fate to at least witness such sights. She saw cavorting young ones climbing onto huge adult boars and jumping into the water. They were all vague and indistinct as shadows. What gave them life were the sounds that rose in the air.

It was a very long time before the boars left. Poonachi thought she would like to stay on inside this forest. There were giant trees everywhere. Plants and creepers grew in abundance. There were ponds to drink from as well as to swim in, rocks on which she could lie down and stretch out. She could keep going in any direction as if through endless space. Would any beasts strike her down, like the wildcat that came and snatched her when she was a baby? Why don't I live here until something like that happens? All kinds of strange ideas occurred to her.

The day dawned slowly. Now the scene at the pond looked different. Flowers stood upright in the water. A flock of birds hovered above in the sky. She got up lazily, put her snout in the pond and sipped some water. It was nectar. She wanted to keep sipping it forever.

Once she left the spot, she remembered the couple, who were probably searching for her everywhere, and became perturbed. What must they be thinking? Let them look for her. Let them wander around. Let them give up their search and go on their way.

She could live without the old couple, but could she bear to live away from Oothan and Uzhumban? Away from those nanny goats, Kaduvayan, Peethan and Porumi as well. Living amidst her own community would give her lasting security. Everything was available in this forest, except her own herd. Could she ever live alone? Weren't the wild boars happy only because they lived together? Would a solitary boar enjoy itself so much? Would she ever find playmates like Oothan and Uzhumban here, in this forest? The more she thought about it, the more fearful she became.

Impelled by the feeling that she must hurry up and reunite with her herd, she ran along every trail she saw, until her legs were tired. Poonachi had no idea where she was going. She seemed to be circling around the same spot. She saw the same sights everywhere. She felt like she was marching in the same place. She ran, nevertheless. She didn't stop even when her legs gave way under her. She drank a couple of mouthfuls whenever she found water and kept running.

At noon, when the sun overhead was stinging hot, she heard the old woman's call: 'Koovey, koovey, koovey!' Poonachi called back immediately and ran in the direction of the call. When both voices merged together, their eyes fell on each other. 'My goddess, my sweet mother, where were you? Why did you lose your way and leave us in the lurch like this?' The old woman kissed the top of Poonachi's head as she spoke. She looked up at the old woman's face and cried out. Both hearts were filled with an immense tenderness. Only then did Poonachi discover that the old man had set out earlier, taking the other goats with him. 'I won't come without Poonachi. I'll find her and bring her with me,' the old woman had told him.

The same night that Poonachi had enjoyed the wild boars' bathing session in the river, the old woman had spent calling out to her without sleeping a wink. Soon after daybreak, she had sent off the old man and then walked around the hill, calling out to Poonachi. For half a day, the old woman's cry had resounded in the forest. Somehow, they had stumbled upon each other. Had the old woman given up on her and gone away, leaving her behind, anything could have happened to Poonachi. She might have been killed and eaten by some predator – or she might have roamed around happily for ever. The old woman had saved her.

The old woman ate nothing that whole day. Whatever had been left of the food in the container, she had sent off with the old man. Had Poonachi not got lost, she would have reached her daughter's house a day earlier. They halted for a night in a village that lay beyond the forest. Many in that village knew her. Lying back in a front pyol, the old woman told the elderly woman of the house the story of how Poonachi had got lost.

The woman asked her, 'You let the kid graze in all kinds of places. What did you have to eat?'

The old woman said, 'To protect this life of mine, do I have to feed it every day? If I only drink water for a day, I won't die, will I?'

Without saying anything, her hostess went inside and brought back a platter filled with rice.

'Is it proper that you come to our house and go to sleep hungry? If you open your mouth and ask for a little rice, will it dent your honour?' she said. The old woman ate without offering any reply.

'The mouth that talks is the same as the one that eats.

Yet, can we talk about anything and everything? Or can we eat anything and everything?' the old woman said.

The woman of the house said that once upon a time, wild hounds, jackals, leopards and herds of deer had lived in that forest. Now, there were only wild boar.

'People keep destroying everything and shoving every last bit into their mouths. How then can anything or anyone survive here apart from human beings? In the end, can even people survive for very long?' she remarked with a sigh.

13

THEY REACHED THE couple's daughter's house at noon on the following day. The front yard was wide and spacious like a threshing floor, with half-a-dozen neem trees at one end. A hut under those trees housed a herd of goats. Poonachi hurried over and joined them. On seeing her, all the goats bleated together to ask after her welfare.

'Don't tell me you roamed the entire forest for this lifeless kid!' the daughter teased the old woman. She had five children of various ages, who kept coming to the hut and playing with the goats.

Except for a solitary goat, the household had only sheep in their pen. The goat had three kids. They were slightly bigger than Uzhumban and Oothan, somewhat smaller than Kaduvayan and Peethan. One was a buck; the other two were does. Poonachi was happy with the sudden increase in the number of her playmates. The story of how she had got lost in the forest and how the old woman found her was recounted in great detail. The old woman had vowed that when Poonachi grew up and delivered a litter, one of her buck kids would be sacrificed to Lord Mesagaran. As she did endless rounds of the forest in search of Poonachi, she had carried this vow of supplication in her heart.

The daughter's house was a thatched shed, just like their own. There were two or three small huts around it. An old couple lived there as well.

Poonachi was happy during their week-long stay in that house. She took a great liking to Poovan, the buck kid. His whole body was white except for a mole-like black patch near the jaw. He had a round face, with a bulging snout. His body was robust and strong. He had grown a fine pair of horns. At first, Poonachi was not sure whether he would want to play with her. After all, she was thin, all black and had a protruding belly. But Poovan was quite amiable.

For some reason, Poovan didn't like Porumi at all. Porumi was constantly trying to attract his attention, crawling over and rubbing against him, but he chose to roam around only with Poonachi. It made her feel proud. She now enjoyed a standing in the herd.

Poovan was keen on playing catch-me-if-you-can. He would ask Poonachi to run, and then chase her. But he wouldn't touch her. He would leap over her and land on the other side. As he leapt through the air with his legs folded back, it looked as if he was flying, and she would gaze upward in wonder. He would torment her by seeming to be in no hurry to touch her. Usually, when she was playing with Oothan and Uzhumban, they would touch her immediately. She was 'it' so often that she hated playing with them. Poovan, on the other hand, gave her so many chances to get away that she didn't mind when he finally touched her. Similarly, whenever Poonachi was about to touch him, he would sidestep her and leap upward. Poonachi would stand outwitted. In the end, however, he would let himself be cornered without making her run around too much.

Only once during that week, behind the cover of palm fronds, did he press his mouth on hers and give her a deep kiss. It tasted delicious to Poonachi. She expected him to kiss her again, whenever the occasion arose, but despite many opportunities, he refrained from doing so. She was rather cut up with him on this score. How could she go and stand before him on her own, raising her mouth to his?

At sunset, when a crimson cloud unfurled in the sky, Poovan played a different game. He approached her gently and rubbed against her body. When she moved closer so that he could caress her some more, he moved away. Poonachi didn't have a rope around her neck yet. At night, she could sleep wherever she wanted. She would go and lie down next to Poovan. It was such a pleasure to sleep next to his body. Reclining on his belly, she felt totally relaxed. Sometimes he curled up with his neck placed on hers. The two strands of his beard tickled her. At the slightest touch of his horn on her body, she felt aroused.

The whole herd was annoyed by this new-found intimacy between her and Poovan, but neither of them was inclined to pay much heed to the others. Poovan showed her many new things to eat. The taste of moonseed creepers, the bitterness of stinkweed flowers and the melting black of wirebush – she came to know them all. Learning that she liked hill mango leaves, he would take her to a place where these could be found. It gave her a deep thrill to watch him as he ate each morsel with relish and returned to slowly chew the cud.

One sweet night, while she lay next to Poovan, with her head resting on him, the two old women sat talking to each other.

The woman of the house said, 'Why don't you stay here for another week? It's not as if you have children back home who are pining for you. If you stay on, I'll have someone to talk to. When you go away, life will seem empty again.'

'What can I do, ayah? I have to worry about my home, don't I? By now the whole house would have turned into a jungle, covered in dust all over. Once I get back, it'll take me four days to put things in order. Do you think a house will keep without people in it? We have just a small piece of land. We can survive only if we look after it. The rains are decreasing every year. Unless we stay put and get some work done, we will have nothing to eat. Anyhow, we can work only so long as we are physically up to it. After that we'll have to come and take refuge here. Where else can we go?' the old woman said.

Only then did Poonachi realise that the plan was to leave the following morning. Without raising her head from Poovan's body, she began to cry. Feeling the wetness of her tears, Poovan shivered. He turned his head and fondly licked her face.

Just then the daughter came to the front yard and said,

'Amma, why don't you leave Poonachi here? We'll bring her up. It's not as if we can't spare a tiny bit of feed for her stomach.'

When she heard this, Poonachi was overjoyed. The idea of going back to their village hadn't occurred to her at all. She had become deeply attached to this household, as if she was going to stay here permanently. But the old woman wouldn't agree.

'To me, Poonachi is like another child. She is in my arms or near my feet all the time. I simply can't live without her. I didn't search for her all over, inside the forest, and bring her back only to leave her here, did I?' the old woman said with finality. Then she added, unable to bear the disappointment on her daughter's face, 'Here, keep Porumi with you. I have two nanny goats, and they are more than enough for me. But this Poonachi has kept me so busy that I wouldn't know what to do without her around.'

From that moment on, Poonachi began to dislike the old woman. Who asked her to come looking for me? She could have left me in the forest. I would have spent my time happily, eating wild creepers and loitering around with wild boars. She didn't let that happen. Now, she won't allow me to stay here with Poovan either. The old wretch. I have to keep falling into her arms, it seems. From now on, I shall avoid being trapped, Poonachi said to herself.

She lay there all night, thinking about many things. At dawn, Poovan moved some distance away, shat and peed. Then he came back and lay beside her with his face against hers. Gently, he pressed his lips to her mouth and gave her a kiss. Poonachi lay still, imagining that his mouth was stuck to hers. She came back to her senses only when the old woman came and tapped her awake. 'How long will you stay here as a guest? Do you have any thought of going back home? Look at you sleeping!' the old woman said and slapped her fondly on the back. Poovan stood facing in a different direction. Poonachi joined her herd reluctantly and took a step forward, then looked back. Poovan was gazing at her with tears in his eyes. Her eyes filled with tears too. The old man whacked her on the back with a long twig. She moved slowly away.

Just then, Poovan cried out and tugged at his tether. Without turning back, Poonachi sensed that the rope had snapped and he was running towards her. For a minute, both of them stood still, next to each other.

The daughter came running behind Poovan and scolded him: 'Oho, you've gone pretty far, haven't you? Snapping your tether and running off? I don't want to lay a hand on you now but tomorrow, I'll bind your neck and forelegs as close together as possible.' She grabbed what remained of his tether and pulled him back. Poonachi immediately stepped back.

'Just look at the cheek of this worm,' the old man said and asked one of his granddaughters to fetch a length of rope. And so, that day, a rope was tied around Poonachi's neck for the first time; once tied, it was never undone.

They kept hearing Poovan's cries even when they were

far away. Poonachi cried out in reply. Kalli, Kaduvayan and Peethan didn't make such a big noise about Porumi being left behind. Let her live happily there, they must have thought. Porumi had her eye on Poovan. Was he likely to be lured to her side? When she thought of the possibility, and of Porumi standing patiently inside the hut, Poonachi's cries became even louder. It seemed to her that Porumi was laughing at her. Poonachi was overcome with anger and loathing for everyone.

'I've never heard such a loud noise from this baby throat. She never cried so loud even when she was lost inside the forest,' the old woman said, amazed.

All along the way, Poonachi thought about Poovan and cried in agony. Her crying subsided gradually but a layer of sorrow came to permanently inhabit her face. She didn't touch any feed during the journey, no matter how delicious or tasty it appeared. Wherever she looked, she saw dense thickets of wirebush. Poovan appeared in their midst, and she heard his cries of despair. The pleasure she had experienced when his lips grazed her face and planted a kiss on her lingered in her mind. She didn't drink a drop of water the whole day. The old woman was both annoyed and sympathetic.

'Look at how saucy she is. She doesn't have even a bit of flesh on her body, but she wants a male partner soon, it seems,' she kept scolding Poonachi all the way home. At one point she said, 'Don't die on me,' and pressed Poonachi's face down into the water. Poonachi drank a few sips reluctantly.

Kaduvayan lingered close to her the whole day. When her eyes fell on him by chance, Poonachi burst into tears. Without saying anything, he touched her face as if to say, 'That's how it is with everything.'

Poonachi remembered the day Kaduvayan had gone away with Pretty Nose and a different herd. She wept even more bitterly.

14

SOMETHING HAPPENED THE next day that caused Poonachi's grief to melt away. On the third day after they set out from Poovan's house, they had halted in an open field on the outskirts of a village. The day was hot. The goats slumped to the ground, tired from grazing and exhausted from the trek. After washing their hands in a channel adjoining the field, the couple opened their bundle of food. Poonachi lay with a scowl on her face and her head stuck between her legs. Her thoughts wandered to what Poovan might be doing at that hour. She wondered if he thought of her at all, or had forgotten her. The old couple were laughing about something. They must be mocking me and laughing at me, thought Poonachi. She gave them an irritated look.

Just then, Oothan and Uzhumban, who were lying behind the couple, got up slowly. They were greatly attracted by the greenery of the fields in the surrounding area. From the time they got here, they had been nibbling at something or the other. Earlier, the old man and his wife had shouted at them and kept them under control. Now it seemed as if they had made a plan to sneak away. It was quite simple, really. A short distance away, groundnut fields stretched as far as the eye could see. Any goat would have been tempted.

There had been groundnut plants in Poovan's village too. The villagers would dry groundnut stalks in a pile and, on the days when they couldn't take the goats out for grazing, they let them feed on these. The leaves and stems of groundnut plants were delicious. Since the goats had never had access to such food in their own village, they had devoured it eagerly. But even in Poovan's village, they'd never had the chance to feed on green stalks.

Poonachi lay there, watching them. If they made the slightest sound, the old man and his wife would spot them. She wondered what she could do to divert their attention. Just then, Oothan and Uzhumban put their mouths to a creeper and began to chew hurriedly. Poonachi watched the spectacle of those dark green tendrils climbing into their mouths, spilling out from the corners and disappearing. Then she saw a man come running towards them from a distance. 'Dhooyi, dhooyi,' he shouted as he swung his arm and threw a stone at them.

The old man and his wife heard the noise and looked back. The stone flew through the air and struck Uzhumban – who had raised his head at the interruption – on the temple. There was a loud scream. Uzhumban's body rose in the air, spun around and dropped inside the field. 'Aiyo!' the old woman shouted as she rushed to Uzhumban and lifted him. Poonachi stood up in fear and cried out. The whole herd was on its feet by now. But none of them could do anything. Uzhumban's life was gone in one stroke. The old woman beat herself on the chest and wailed.

The farmer hadn't expected this either. He had flung the stone only with the aim of chasing away the kids who were feeding on his crop. Had Uzhumban not raised his head, there would have been no chance of a hit. Poonachi wept inconsolably, wishing that the stone had struck her temple and she had died instead of Uzhumban.

The old man shouted at the farmer in anger, but he replied calmly, 'Would you stand by and watch your groundnut crop being eaten? Only the farmer knows the value of a crop. What would a goatherd know?'

'What a fine buck he was. We looked after him for a year. These animals are our livelihood. What do we do now?' the old man fumed.

Meanwhile, five or six men turned up from the neighbouring fields. Everyone had something to say. These were wayfarers; those were locals. These were two oldies; those were many. That apart, who was to blame for the incident? Was it wrong to have travelled here? Was it wrong to have sat in the shade? Was it wrong that the kids went off to graze? Was it wrong that the farmer threw a stone? Was it wrong that Uzhumban raised his head? Everything happened by chance. If you called it wrong, then everything was wrong.

But the villagers did right by the old man. What was dead couldn't be brought back to life. So what was to be done, they asked. The kid could be butchered for meat.

However many portions it might yield, it was the farmer's responsibility to sell them to the local villagers. The hide could be sold separately. They could convert the dead kid into cash and give it to the old man. What else could be done? If this was not acceptable, the old man could take the body and leave. He had let the kid graze in the field, and the farmer could not but chase it away. The old man agreed.

With a hand on her head, the old woman moaned: 'Mesayya, we came to the festival only because we have faith in you. If you inflict such big losses on us, how will we poor folk survive?' Both parties decided that they would not take the matter to the government or the courts. Once they reached home, the kid's number would be presented at the government office and it would be recorded that he had caught a disease and died during their journey to another village. The old man would arrange this.

They brought Uzhumban's body to the shade. There was a big swelling on the spot where the stone had struck his head. Otherwise, not even a small bruise was found on his body. Through open lids, Uzhumban's eyes stared fixedly ahead. Was it a sin to have craved for a mouthful of groundnut stalk? Should he have paid for it with his life? All the goats stood together, on one side. Oothan's legs were still shaking. He had seen the end of life from up close. How would he ever forget Uzhumban, who had been his constant companion all this while? Stunned, Oothan moved closer to his mother. Later, the entire herd of goats stood watching as Uzhumban's carcass was cut, hacked and divided into portions. If the villagers were to do the same to all the goats standing there, what could they do to stop it? Out of his severed head, Uzhumban's eyes stared at them for a very long time. Unable to look at those eyes or look away, Poonachi stood still, feeling a great emptiness within. As she watched one who had always run with them being reduced gradually to a few portions of meat, she asked herself seriously, Why should I live anymore?

The villagers offered a portion of Uzhumban's meat to the old couple. The old woman refused, saying she was dead against taking it. The villagers collected money for the portions and gave it to the couple.

They spent the night in the pyol of the local temple. Many locals came by to greet them and inquire after their welfare. The old man retired early and went to sleep. Sniffling now and again, the old woman repeated their story tirelessly to anyone who asked. 'Such a pity that the creature was fated to die this way,' she lamented frequently. The story of how Poonachi had got lost kept getting into the conversation too. Several old women from the village met and talked to her, and offered consolation.

Those who had bought the meat and cooked it told her, 'I'll bring you a little. Will you eat?'

'I brought him up like a baby,' the old woman said. 'Do I have the devil's heart that I would consume my own child?'

Even then, some people persisted.

'What's the big problem, ayah? Don't we eat animals that we sacrifice to God? Think of it that way,' they said.

'When we offer a sacrifice, God takes the life and gives us the refuse. But our kid is alive in every bit of this meat. How can a mother have the heart to eat her own son?' asked the old woman.

They listened to her and agreed.

'Pity the person who suffered the loss, but it's no gain for the one who got the meat,' another old woman said.

15

On the fifteenth night after their return from the pilgrimage, Poonachi attained puberty. Throughout those fifteen days, she had only Poovan on her mind. Uzhumban's frozen eyes would appear too, every now and then.

'The difficulties of the dead leave along with them, those of the living are here to stay,' the old woman said often. The thought kept recurring in Poonachi's mind too. Had they not gone on the pilgrimage, they wouldn't be in this trouble now. But it was only because they had travelled that she had got to explore the forest and spend at least a few happy days with Poovan. The moonlit tableau of the wild boars cavorting in the pond was etched in her mind. Every time she closed her eyes, the scene would unfold. What a miracle, she thought to herself.

The two kisses planted by Poovan lingered on her mouth. She thought about it all the time, and her happiness playing with Poovan. She imagined him flying through the air and leaping over her. There were so many moments she could recall with pleasure. Why then did the mind always blow up and despair over sad events? Each time she thought of the happy times, her mind would be filled with joy. To everyone's surprise, she would jump and run around in the pasture.

Oothan asked her once in anger: 'Are you even a little sad that Uzhumban is dead?'

'Is he going to wake from the dead if I worry about him? Of course we must remember him. But if we think about him all the time, how are we to live?' Poonachi asked him in return, feeling rather proud of her own profundity.

Now Oothan went everywhere with her. He wasn't very refined. When they were playing, he would suddenly rub his snout against her. She didn't like it one bit, and her thoughts would fly to Poovan. Although Oothan had his eye on Poonachi, she thought of him only as a playmate.

Then, one night, Poonachi sensed a vast change come over her body. She felt acute pain in her lower abdomen. A while later, something seemed to slide out of her stomach and ooze from her vagina. All at once, her heart was filled with Poovan and she moaned without realising it. To the old woman, it sounded like a cry induced by a pleasurable pain, and it made no sense to her. Despite her familiarity with the mating calls of numberless goats, she thought of Poonachi as an infant who had yet to be weaned. Even the affection Poonachi had developed for Poovan was construed by her as friendship between playmates.

'I don't know what has happened to her. Let me light the lamp and check. Get up and come with me,' she called to her husband for help.

The old man had grasped the nature of Poonachi's call.

'All she wants is a mate. As you grow older, you seem to understand less and less,' he said.

'Really? The kid needs a mate, does she?' Laughing, the old woman went over to Poonachi. Her fingers found the sticky fluid oozing from her vagina. Poonachi's body was covered in gooseflesh; she felt cold. She yearned for the old woman to touch her more intimately. Looking at the way she stood there, crouched, the old woman said, 'Ah, yes, it's happened early.'

That whole night the couple's conversation revolved around what they should do to mate Poonachi and where they should take her. 'There's a buck in our daughter's house, but what's the use? Even if people are willing to help you out, they need to be close by,' the old woman said in an aggrieved tone.

Poonachi listened to her with keen interest but understood quite quickly that meeting Poovan would be next to impossible. She wondered what it would be like if Poovan was with her just now.

'We have Oothan, but he is so small he can't even reach a creeper yet. Do you think a buck might come to the pasture?' the old woman asked.

'Do you want her mated right away? Let's wait for one more season. The kid's hips aren't strong enough yet,' the old man said.

'Hmm. She'll start calling out again before a week goes by. We can't possibly live here listening to that noise all the time. Try to find a buck from somewhere,' the old woman said.

After a great deal of discussion, they identified a neighbouring village where it was possible to hire the mating services of a buck for a fee.

Early the next morning, the old man caught hold of Poonachi and took her there. She ran swiftly along with him. She was dying to see Poovan. If not Poovan, she would get someone like him. What would this new one be like? Would he have a round face, like a cat? Or a gaunt face with sunken cheeks? Would he plant kisses on her like Poovan had? Would he amuse and entertain her? Her imagination ran wild as she followed the old man.

They reached the place before dawn. Goats loitered inside a large enclosure. Poonachi was surprised to find that just like for sheep, there was a pen for goats too. A youthful looking fellow arrived and opened the enclosure.

'Why, thatha! The kid looks like an insect. Can she withstand this?'

'She may be small like an insect and feeble too, but for the pleasure of mating she will withstand anything,' the old man replied.

The young man opened the enclosure and led out an old ram. Exhaustion from having impregnated countless nanny goats was etched on his face. His body was huge. Displaying a complete lack of interest, he came over and stood near Poonachi. She turned her face away, disgusted. With her eyes closed, she trembled. A moment later, she felt a big load being mounted on her back. Unable to bear the weight, she collapsed to the ground in less than a second. Semen spurted uselessly from the ram's penis.

'Why did you let go of her, thatha?' the young man said.

'Hey, bring a young buck if you have one. The kid is very young, isn't she?'

'You are the one who said that she would withstand anything. Now you want a young buck? Where do I go to find one? I thought you were experienced and listened to you. Look at him now, he has wasted his semen. All right, I'll let another buck have a go, but you have to pay for two, is that clear?' the young man said.

'Sure, I'll pay for four. Even if she can withstand a lot, everything should have a limit, right? This one is such an ancient ram,' the old man laughed.

To replace the ancient ram, they brought one that was merely old. The goat was so tall that when he came over, only his legs were visible. 'Put her in a brace and hold on,' the young man said.

The old man pushed Poonachi inside a brace made of logs tied on both sides and a wooden barrier in front to prevent the animal from moving forward. There was a plank laid inside. After lifting Poonachi on to the plank, the old man drew a rope through the barrier in front and fastened it around her neck so she couldn't move. Then he stood behind her, lifted her tail up and held her body firmly in place. The young man released the ram. For a second, Poonachi felt as if a hot rod had been inserted into her stomach and pulled out immediately; that was all. It was enough to make her feel small and humiliated. After paying the young man, the old man walked home with Poonachi in tow.

Poonachi was disgusted with the whole world. What was the connection between a faceless old ram and her body? It was beyond her understanding. Did the joy of mating amount to no more than this? It would have been the same even with Poovan. Why was I born into this world? Poonachi wondered, for the first time in her life.

When she roamed the pasture with the other goats, Oothan caught the scent of her heat and followed behind. A few other bucks rubbed against her as well. She didn't lift her tail for any of them. She was tempted to do Oothan a favour. But it would take some time for the bruise from the morning to heal; she didn't need another at this time.

Poor Oothan. If she allowed him today, tomorrow he might end up in the same condition as Kaduvayan. She walked on with a subdued heart and body, listlessly picking at the feed and drinking water. She doubted whether she could recall a single happy moment anymore. If she had mated with Poovan, it would have been a happy event. Why was she deprived of it then? Why hadn't she come of age when she was still in Poovan's village? It felt strange to think that a dried-up old goat had invaded her body. Chcha, it was no good brooding over it. Poonachi shook her head to free herself of the memory and tried to divert her attention to other matters.

16

THE OLD WOMAN was keeping a steady eye on Poonachi. In a month, Poonachi's udder had sagged a little lower. The matted hair on her skin fell away and she looked more fecund.

'The kid must be pregnant,' she told her husband.

Poonachi noticed many changes in her body. She began to feel as though she was carrying a big load in her stomach. She was ravenously hungry all the time. The old woman gave her plenty to eat, and Poonachi kept eating. The food she had been given when she was a kid – water in which oilcake had been soaked overnight – was offered to her again. The old woman gathered tender shoots and leaves from all over and brought them home for Poonachi.

When she returned home from the pasture, Poonachi would rush to find out what novel delicacy the old woman had brought for her. The old woman had kept aside a separate basket for Poonachi. One day, Poonachi found in it a pile of unripe babul fruit, evergreen and shiny as pearls. On another day she found a heap of lemongrass. Foliage from gulmohur trees, hill mango leaves and wild cockscomb plants – Poonachi enjoyed them all. No one knew when and where the old woman went to collect these things. Poonachi thrived, consuming everything that came her way.

The rains that year were nothing to speak about. There was a light drizzle now and again, a mere sprinkle in the front yard. During the season, it rained a little over a couple of days. There would be no shortage of drinking water, but farming operations were disrupted. Farmers planted their crop based on the availability of water, harvested whatever came up, and got by on it.

The old woman took care of Poonachi like her own child. She hadn't paid so much attention even to her daughter when she came home for her first delivery. Solely to meet their commitment of looking after Poonachi, the old man took Kaduvayan and Peethan to the market fair and sold them. The hut and the front yard now wore a deserted look.

Soon after this, Kalli became pregnant. Oothan was castrated. Now there were only four of them left. No one played about. There was no leaping and jumping around. It seemed as if time lay inert, like oilcake. There was no chance that Kaduvayan and Peethan would be still alive. The old man said he had sold them to a butcher. In their daughter's house, Porumi would most likely be pregnant by now. Was Poovan still there? He may have mated with Porumi. After being so affectionate and loving with Poonachi, would Poovan do that? But then, despite loving Poovan, she'd had to lift her tail for an old ram, hadn't she? How could Porumi be the lesser mate? She was the same age as Poovan. But for some reason, he had been more loving towards Poonachi. That was all.

It was a good opportunity for Oothan. He was the only kid still suckling at Semmi's udder. The old woman didn't let him drink all the milk, though. When she untied him in the morning, he would go quickly to Semmi, grab her udder and suckle. Once her teats were flowing with milk, the old woman would drag Oothan away and tie him up. She would then milk Semmi two or three times until her vessel was full. Oothan's chance to feed came while grazing in the pasture. There he would suckle whenever he pleased. Standing with her legs apart and eyes closed, Semmi would suckle him while she slowly chewed the cud.

But she didn't always tolerate Oothan's butting of her udder. She would kick him in the face and move away. At any rate, Oothan suckled at least three or four times during the day, even if he was not allowed to suckle at night.

The old woman gave a small quantity of goat milk to her husband every day. A girl turned up daily from a remote farm to buy the rest. From her brief conversations with the girl, the old woman gathered that someone in her house was ailing and goat milk was part of the cure. It brought in some extra money for the old woman.

Right from the beginning of the fourth month of her pregnancy, Poonachi could barely do anything. Walking for a few minutes made her gasp for breath. She had to lie down and rest every so often. She couldn't stand and graze for long. Just getting to the pasture required enormous effort.

Seeing her difficulties, the old man told his wife, 'Let her graze somewhere close by.' It had rained a few days earlier and grass had sprouted everywhere. But the fresh blades tasted bitter. She couldn't eat more than a couple of mouthfuls.

The old woman began to take Poonachi to a nearby field and tether her at the edge. She would keep the rope short to make sure that the standing crop was beyond her reach. Poonachi would graze as far as she could reach and then lie down. The old woman would check on her every now and then. Sometimes she would bring rice water and make Poonachi drink it. Water in which cooked millet had been soaked was very tasty. If that came Poonachi's way, she would drink till she was about to burst. Water from brown millet was also a favourite. Finger millet, though, tasted insipid and bland.

'You always want something tasty, don't you? If you are so picky when you are pregnant, what will happen to your kids?' The old woman rebuked her fondly with a tap on the cheek. She imagined that she was actually ministering to her daughter.

The old woman had noted the date on which Poonachi was mated with the old ram. It was her job to recite the calculation every night to the old man. 'Eight and seven days are fifteen. Two fifteens are thirty. Four thirties are one hundred and twenty. It's been a hundred and twenty days now,' she said one day. Fifteen days more, and Poonachi would be ready to deliver, they concluded.

One night the old woman asked her husband, 'Bakasuran

told you she would have seven kids in a litter. Is that really true? From the size of her belly, it looks like there are three. When both her hips are swollen, I can see three heads.'

'That's what he claimed. I've never seen a goat deliver seven kids in a litter. I've seen them birth four or five, sure. Like you said, this one is set for three. Raising three kids is a fair job, don't you think?'

'Yes. Let me ask you something that's been bothering me all these years. And please tell me the truth without getting angry,' the old woman said.

'Why should I lie to you? Ask me anything,' the old man said cheerfully.

'Did Bakasuran really give you this kid? Or did you see her lying near a bush and bring her home?' the old woman said.

'Go on, woman! You never believe me. And it's not like you're going to trust me now, when our time is nearly up. But I'll tell you anyway. So, listen. It was the hour of sunset. In the distance, I saw a shadow moving. It looked like a tall, robust tree. As the sun goes down, shadows get longer, don't they? I thought this shadow was like that. As it came slowly towards me, I narrowed my eyes and looked. The man was very tall, almost one-half the height of a palm tree. If you had seen him, you would have thought he was an ogre and peed down your leg.'

Poonachi's mind was full of questions as she listened to him recount the story. How did I come into Bakasuran's hands? Where is my mother? Where do these demons live?

Will I ever see my mother? I wasn't so big, was I, that Bakasuran couldn't take care of me? But who knows what hardships he faced.

Just as the old woman had calculated, Poonachi went into labour one rainy evening. Mild in the beginning, the pain intensified rapidly. She kept lying down and getting up, unable to settle in one place. The old woman came in and put something inside the basket. Poonachi didn't even feel like checking what it might be. She cried out in anguish. Since it was her first pregnancy, the old woman knew that delivery was going to be difficult. But such severe pain? Something must be wrong with Poonachi, she thought.

She waited patiently until darkness fell and everything was quiet and still. Then she untied Poonachi's rope. Poonachi went out of the hut and lay down at the entrance. Then she got up. She lay down under the old woman's cot. She got up. She lay down beside the pile of dry leaves that the old man had heaped in a corner. She got up. She went and lay down next to Kalli, who nuzzled and consoled her with a gentle bleat. Poonachi got up. She lay down between Oothan and his mother. Sensing her agony, they looked at her with sympathy and compassion. She got up. There was no help for it. Regardless of whether she cried, rolled around, lay down or got up, she alone had to deliver the kids. Others could bring her no relief.

Made nervous by Poonachi's restlessness, the old woman told her husband, 'Go to the village and bring the midwife. I can't bear to watch her suffering like this. Maybe some kid in there has turned upside down.'

'You don't even have the patience to wait a while. As if she was your own daughter or something,' the old man muttered to himself as he prepared to leave.

The old woman guessed the route he had taken from the sound of the dogs barking. Stroking Poonachi's head fondly, she spoke consoling words to her: 'Just hold on for some time. The midwife will be here soon.'

The old man seemed to have broadcast the saga of Poonachi's labour pains to everyone along the way. Five or six women turned up at the couple's shed. With the sound of people talking and shouting animatedly, the front yard turned lively. Some of them recalled past incidents in their homes which involved severe labour pains. Their presence was a huge comfort to the old woman. She lit a big earthen lamp and kept it in a safe spot in the front yard where it wouldn't be put out by the wind. She decided that moving around so much wasn't doing Poonachi any good, so she tied her to a leg of the cot. Now Poonachi kept lying down and getting up in the same spot.

'Here we are, chatting about what's gone by, while that poor thing is still suffering,' a woman said.

'Yes, we learn about fever and headache only when they affect us personally,' another woman agreed.

'Ada, only the egg-laying hen knows the pain of an inflamed asshole,' a different woman added.

Amid the banter, the sound of the old man approaching from a distance could be heard. It seemed the midwife was coming with him. The midwife was said to be lucky with his hands. Regardless of the kind of problem a goat might have, he would resolve it in no time. After rubbing castor oil on his hands, he would insert his hand inside the goat's vagina and, without hurting the mother or the kids, he would pull the babies out, one after another. His arrival gave the old woman confidence. As the two men approached closer and closer, Poonachi's cries grew louder. The old woman ran to her to find out what had happened.

Poonachi, who had been on her feet until then, was lying on her back with her hind legs splayed, straining hard and pushing. The old woman brought the lamp's flame closer to her. The first kid slid out and dropped like a ball of flour, with a thin covering of mucus. The old woman picked it up, wiped away the mucus and let it breathe.

'There is a time for everything. No point in being in a hurry,' someone said.

17

AT THE SAME speed with which the first kid was pushed out, other kids followed, one after another. Four kids in all. Poonachi slowly tried to get up. The old woman extended a hand and lifted her up. Once she was on her feet, Poonachi licked her kids all over, first to remove the mucus covering, then to wipe the wetness from their skin. Each kid was as fat as a grub worm.

'Hey, if there were four kids in her belly, they *had* to be tiny,' someone said.

The midwife came to the front yard and saw the kids. He lifted Poonachi's tail and looked at her vagina. 'There are more kids inside,' he said. 'What!' The villagers around him were shocked. But it wasn't a shock for the old man and his wife. After all, Bakasuran had told him that she would yield seven kids in a litter.

The midwife was not an ordinary person. He came from a line of midwives. He must have been less than fifty years of age. Nevertheless, he was quite experienced, having assisted his father in performing deliveries from an early age. The couple believed his words must be true. However, Poonachi was busy licking her four kids, as though it was all over and done with. Any onlooker would have thought the midwife's prediction wrong. It seemed that the heaviness of Poonachi's belly had reduced and her stomach was empty again. But in the next few minutes she experienced another series of spasms and wanted to lie down again.

As she stretched out, she glanced at the kids crawling on the ground near her. The next moment, without realising it, she gave a push. Two kids slid out, one after another. Poonachi stood up again, on her own. One of the women who had crowded around Poonachi said, 'How strange is this? She is pushing them out like turds.' Poonachi licked the two new kids all over. The midwife touched and pressed her belly with his fingers. He examined her uterus. It was still sticky. 'That's it,' he said. The old woman was wiping the mucus covering on the body of each kid. Poonachi kept licking the kids continuously to dry their skin.

Six kids, of whom four were bucks and two were does. Four of them were pitch black like Poonachi; the other two were brown. It was a joyful sight, the kids wriggling and crying by the lamplight. The old woman lifted the lamp along with the boom and looked at each kid under the light. The eyes of the black kids glittered. Everyone came close and gawked at them, then they sat in the backyard and resumed chatting. 'Six kids, you have to look after them well,' the midwife told the old woman and prepared to leave.

All at once Poonachi lay down again; again, a push. Another kid slid out and dropped to the ground. Following

115

this, her umbilical cord began to unravel. Thus proven wrong, the midwife was struck dumb for a few minutes. Since the umbilical cord was hanging out, it was certain that there would be no more kids in the litter. He was hesitant to say it, though. 'Seven?' Everyone else was as stunned as the midwife.

'Bakasuran really was the embodiment of truth,' the old man told himself. Now, finally, the old woman believed that her husband had told her the truth, not a story.

The seventh kid looked exactly like Poonachi. She was of the same size, shape and colour that Poonachi had been when the old man came home on that distant evening and placed her in his wife's hands. Poonachi may have been the seventh kid in her mother's litter, the old woman thought.

'You've had such a stroke of luck,' a woman said. She spoke for everyone present there, the jealousy apparent in her voice.

'Even Mesagaran can't predict the luck of rainfall or offspring,' the midwife said. His words were a way of coping with the failure of his verdict.

Poonachi licked her last kid all over. Her tongue was dry. The old woman lit the mud stove and boiled water on it. She took a measure of pearl millet from the vat and soaked it in water. When the water became lukewarm, she took it off the stove and replaced it with the millet. She washed and scrubbed down Poonachi with warm water. Then she cleaned and rinsed all the bloodstains on Poonachi's body.

As he was about to leave, the midwife said, 'Seven kids

in a litter is a miracle. Go immediately and inform the government. If you go tomorrow, they will ask questions. How can a goat birth seven kids? What chicanery have you been up to? Where did you steal them from? No matter what you say, they will call you a liar and put you in jail.'

'It's true, 'pa. Leave right now. These days, even if you fart, you have to register it with the government,' a woman said.

'We might even have a law which says you can only fart twice in a day,' another woman said.

Approaching the servants of the regime was always a big problem for the old man. He was frightened and nervous even of an employee from the lowest rung of the ladder. He couldn't possibly ask his wife to go in his place this time, so he pleaded with the midwife to accompany him. The authorities would believe the midwife's testimony. Once the two men set out, the visitors followed them out. The old woman, Poonachi and the kids were the only ones left.

Now each of the kids tried to slowly get up and stand on its feet. The old woman was afraid that, in the dark of the night, some predator might sneak in like the wildcat that had come to grab Poonachi. She had to be alert. Feeling the weight of responsibility on her shoulders, she busied herself with work. She spread the cooked millet on a winnowing pan and let it cool. Then she took the vessel containing water that had been drained from the cooked millet and placed it on the hot coals in the stove. If all the kids got up and started walking, how was she going to find them in the dark? She felt bewildered.

She held the winnowing pan with the cooked millet in front of Poonachi. The moment she smelled it, Poonachi felt ravenously hungry. The old woman had trouble holding the pan steady as she gobbled up the warm millet. A whole measure was devoured in no time at all. Then the old woman brought the millet water from the stove. After drinking it, Poonachi's deflated belly seemed to swell once again. She felt stronger. The umbilical cord which had been hanging out of her uterus slid down and dropped by itself. The old woman picked it up, put it in a basket, and covered it with a lid. When the old man returned, she would ask him to hang it from a pala tree. Then milk would flow generously from Poonachi's udder.

The kids kept getting up, falling down and stumbling. She picked them up, one by one, carried them to Poonachi and put their mouths to a teat. The moment an infant's mouth touched her teat, Poonachi's whole body tingled. Unable to bear the sensation, she kicked out with her leg. 'You tingle even when you're feeding your own kid, do you?' the old woman scolded.

Poonachi pressed her feet gently on the ground and stood up. As each kid got hold of a teat and suckled, the tingling sensation subsided. After the kids had suckled a few mouthfuls, their mouths got tired and they refused to suckle anymore. By the time she got all the seven kids, one by one, to suckle, the old woman was exhausted.

Can this Poonachi suckle all the seven kids? What if she runs short of milk? When each kid runs in a different direction, how will I catch them and keep them in one place? The old woman's mind was filled with questions.

She put all the kids in a big basket and closed it. Immediately, Poonachi started crying. The old woman opened the basket and kept it in front of Poonachi. 'Um … um … um,' she called out to her kids and they answered back. Just when the old woman was wondering where to put the kids so that she could keep an eye on them, she heard her husband's footsteps in the front yard.

He reported that the official for ear-piercing had been informed. 'How dare you come to my house?' the official had yelled when they had asked to meet him. He had slammed the door shut and gone off inside. Later, after they had explained the matter courteously to his wife, she had relayed it to him and brought him back. When they told him about the seven kids, he simply couldn't believe it. 'Seven, is it? Really?' he asked them many times. Even after the midwife confirmed it, the official refused to believe them.

'Seven kids, huh?' he said. 'This is a miracle even for the government. The higher authorities must be informed.' He told them he would come to see the kids the following morning and made a note in his calendar.

18

THE COUPLE COULDN'T sleep that night. 'Get some shut-eye,' they kept telling each other, but neither of them slept a wink. Once every short while, the old woman gave Poonachi something to eat. She made the kids suckle two or three times. They talked endlessly about Poonachi's feed and about milk for the kids. They also talked about how they had happened to witness a miracle in their lifetime. They reminded each other that they should never open their mouths about Bakasuran to anyone. Why had he chosen them to receive the gift of Poonachi?

The old woman could not see him as a demon at all. 'Lord Mesagaran himself must have come in the form of that giant,' she said.

'Maybe,' her husband replied.

The day broke. They could now see the kids properly in the morning light. Of the seven kids, four were bucks, two black and two brown. All three does, including the youngest of the seven, were black. The five black kids looked exactly the same. The old woman tried to distinguish between the bucks and the does, but it wasn't easy. Later, while she was milking Semmi, she thought she could get her to suckle some of Poonachi's kids. They wouldn't have any problem with milk today. The kids only needed to wet their bellies and they would fall sleep. She could try to get Semmi to suckle them a couple of days from now.

As the news spread, everyone in the village came by to look at the kids. Each of the visitors picked them up and fondled them, sometimes roughly. Fortunately, as soon as news spread about the arrival of the ear-piercing official, all the visitors slipped away one by one.

When the sun had risen to a man's height above the horizon, the official arrived on horseback. A huge crowd followed him. Seeing the horse and the crowd of people, the goats were frightened and cried out, tugging at their ropes and rolling on the ground. The old man and his wife were gripped by a terrible fear too. The enquiry began.

'What's your name?' asked the official. The old man and his wife told him.

'Bring the tokens,' the official said.

The old woman rushed into the shed and, after a brief search, fetched the tokens from inside a pot where they were stashed. The tokens, which were round and bore the official seal of the government, had turned black from lying inside the pot for a long time. The numbers engraved on them were not legible.

'Are they genuine?' asked the junior official who had accompanied his superior.

'Yes, sir,' the old woman said. The official scraped the surface of the tokens and examined them closely.

'You should preserve them properly,' he said. Then the high-level inquiry started.

'Is it true that there were seven kids?' the official asked while staring at the sky.

'They are here in the basket. Take a look, sir,' the old woman said, showing him the basket.

'Answer the question. Is it true?'

'It's true, sir.'

'Count them and verify that there are seven,' the official told an assistant who was standing next to him. The assistant put his hand inside the basket and counted the kids one by one. 'Seven, sir. It's true,' he said. The official noted this down in the register.

'When did the incident happen?'

'What's that, sir?'

'When did the incident take place?'

The assistant came over to the old woman and said, 'When did the goat deliver the litter? That's what he is asking, 'ma.'

'Last night,' the old woman said.

'At what time?' The official's gaze bumped against the roof of the shed and halted there.

'After eating my meal, I pulled out my cot, thinking that I'd go to sleep. That's when Poonachi started to cry. Then, within about three hours, the delivery happened, sir,' the old woman explained.

The midwife stepped forward and said, 'You can put it down as nine o' clock, sir.'

The official allotted numbers for all the seven kids. Because their ears were still soft, he said he would return in a week to carry out the ear-piercing. Information had been provided to the higher authorities and if someone came to inquire, they should tell him exactly what they had said to him, he cautioned. When the officer was about to leave, someone came running up to him. It seemed he was the informer whose job it was to send a report to the government.

He asked the official, 'Do you think there is some cheating involved in this miracle?'

'I doubt there is anything of that kind. At any rate, we will know the truth only after we conduct a top-level inquiry,' the official replied.

The informer came to the old man and his wife and asked them, 'They say it happened in the normal way, is it true?'

'Of course it's true. Do you want to see?' the old woman said.

'How did it happen?'

'We can only ask Mesagaran.'

'When the seven kids were delivered, what was your state of mind?'

'I didn't birth those seven kids, did I, thambi? It was the goat that did.'

'That's right. What was *your* state of mind then?'

'What does that mean – state of mind?'

'I am asking: what did you think at the time?'

'I prayed that the delivery should happen without any loss of life, that the mother and kids should come out of it without any injury or defect.'

'I don't mean that, 'ma. I am asking you: how did you *feel*?'

Just then the old man intervened: 'We felt very happy, thambi. Will that do?'

'Hmm. That's just what I was asking. What are you going to do from now on?'

'We will bring up the kids.'

'How will you bring them up?'

'By giving them milk and feeding them, of course.'

'How will you give milk to so many kids? You can appeal to the government to sanction a grant for this purpose, can't you?'

'Won't the government get angry, thambi?'

'No, no, they won't. If you ask the government nicely, they will never get angry.'

'All right, thambi. It will be good for us if the government gives some assistance like you said. But when they offer help, won't they also take the kids away?'

'No, they won't. One last question: what would you like to say through this interview?'

'What should we like to say?'

'Something like: "We are raising goats that can deliver seven kids at one go. Everyone should raise these types of goats. Only then will the country develop rapidly and become a superpower." Shall we say that you are asking everyone to raise goats?'

'All right. We can say that.'

Over the next few days, government informers claiming to be from this village or that kept arriving to visit them. They always started: 'Tell us about yourself.'

News of the miracle of the seven kids spread through the territories under the government. There were many people who wished to see them. They started heading there with bundles of food for the journey. Some brought a portrait artist with them. They sat among the kids and asked him to draw a portrait. Poonachi grew very tired from having to frequently turn this way and that, and standing on her feet for long hours. She didn't know why so many people came swarming to the hut.

She couldn't even suckle her kids. When the visitors picked up the kids and fondled them, it seemed as if they might strangle them to death. Some had brought children with them. They hugged the kids tight and pressed them to their bodies. To Poonachi they seemed like ogres who had come to murder her kids.

One day, when he was fed up of answering questions from visitors and showing them around, the old man said to his wife, 'Shall we give Poonachi to the government?'

She replied, 'No need for that. From tomorrow, we will charge a penny per person for seeing the miracle. This is what they do at the Mesagaran temple: whenever there is a crowd, they charge a small amount.'

'That's right. If it's free, people will come in droves. If there is a charge, they'll run away,' the old man said.

Perumal Murugan

The next morning, the old man built a thatched barrier all around the hut that housed Poonachi and her kids. A few hours after daybreak, a crowd turned up. When they were told that there was a charge for seeing the kids, many of them backed out. A few paid the charge reluctantly, came into the hut, and looked at the kids. Four days later, there was no sign nor sound of strangers in the hut's vicinity.

19

POONACHI AND THE old woman had to toil hard to bring up the seven kids. No matter how much she ate, it wasn't enough for Poonachi; all the nourishment was being drained out through her udder. Her kids were suckling constantly. She stood with her legs wide apart almost all the time. The old woman roamed everywhere, picked up all kinds of feed and offered them to Poonachi. Raising the kids kept her busy day and night. It was no easy task to get Semmi to suckle the kids. She cried and fled whenever anyone approached her. Semmi had once suckled Poonachi; now she had to suckle Poonachi's kids.

The old man would hold Semmi's head, pry her mouth open, put his hand inside and firmly hold down her tongue and lower jaw with his fingers. Unable to break free, Semmi would stand still. Holding her hind legs wide apart, the old woman would let the kids through to suckle. She had divided them into two groups: four of them for Poonachi to suckle, and the remaining three for Semmi. It was a tussle every day, in the morning and evening. Just as she had done with Poonachi, she fed the kids rice water through a feeding tube.

She also made them drink oilcake water. The kids crawled and played around in the front yard. Everyone had to tread cautiously. If someone were to step on one of them, even lightly, it would mean the end of that little thing.

One night, the old woman said, 'Taking care of this miracle is ruining our lives.'

'A miracle if we are far away, a nuisance from up close,' the old man said with a sigh.

'Yes, why did that Bakasuran give us this wretched creature? Why impose a load on people who can't carry it?'

'I've been thinking about it too. It makes no sense.'

'Maybe he was a messenger sent by Mesagaran to tell us something?'

'Are we so important that God would want to send us a message?'

'True.'

'We could have given the kids away and kept only the two does.'

'We didn't think of that, did we? Even we poor folk want to keep these luckless kids with us. No matter how much you give to this heart, it will never be enough.'

'Say that again.'

'No matter how much you give to this heart, it will never be enough.'

'Did he give us Poonachi just to make us understand this?'

'What do we gain by such understanding?'

'True.'

'Should he make us suffer so much, just to get us to

understand? If we had known this earlier, we could have passed her on to someone else and moved on. Why do we need to understand anything?'

'If she delivers seven the next time, we'll give them away.'

'Should we keep this cursed thing till the next litter?'

'We have to. She is an asset that someone has left in our care. Come what may, we should never sell the principal. If Bakasuran comes back in a year or two and wants to know how well we are looking after her, what will we tell him?'

'We'll tell him that we sold her and spent the money.'

'But we don't have the heart to do it.'

'We are not his bonded slaves, are we?'

Their conversation went on in this vein for some more time, but they were unable to come to a decision. They had faced difficulties all their lives. Nothing could end their suffering. Even the rain was playing hide-and-seek with them. What could they do? How could poor people like them eke out a living?

Poonachi had grown even thinner. There was a dent in her stomach. She had sunken eyes. She didn't even have the strength to open her mouth and bleat. Whenever her kids reached for her udder now, she kicked out with her legs and started running. She rarely stood still for them. Left with no alternative, the kids started nibbling grass.

Meanwhile, Semmi became pregnant. Oothan was sold. Kalli delivered a small litter of two kids. Looking at the two kids, each suckling from a teat, and the mother goat standing with her eyes closed, chewing the cud, Poonachi was envious. Such good fortune had never come her way.

She wondered sometimes whether her teats had actually been torn off because of all the grabbing and pulling by her kids. Her udder was so inflamed she imagined that blood, not milk, dripped from her teats.

Somehow her kids managed to grow. Poonachi would look wistfully at them as they jumped about and played in the front yard. While all the other goats in the pasture were either white or brown, her brood moved as a separate group, leaping about as though darkness itself was on the move. She loved the idea of a pasture filled with the lives she had birthed. After two or three more deliveries, the whole place would be teeming with her progeny, she thought proudly. But she also wondered whether she would be able to endure the ordeal of more deliveries.

There was a huge demand for all the three does from the litter. Owners of large pens came to meet the old man and convey their interest. Some women approached the old woman, served up some sweet talk and then placed a request with her as they were leaving: 'You *have* to give one of the three does to me.' However, everyone was aware that they couldn't raise these kids on their own.

Since the does came from a line that delivered seven kids in a litter, the number of goats in the owner's pen would go up very fast. But there were many affluent men in the old man's community, the Asuras, who owned a large number of goats and had servants to graze them. They would have no difficulty in arranging milk for the kids or looking after them.

The old man and his wife were in a quandary, unable to decide who they should give the kids to.

One night the old man said, 'In a month, it will be time for the festival in our daughter's village. How can we travel if we have to drive these kids along?'

The old woman thought it over. Last year's journey had turned out to be an ordeal. Poonachi getting trapped inside the forest, Uzhumban's death, and the hardships they had suffered because of those incidents were still fresh in her mind. But they couldn't call off their visit to their daughter's house. If they went during the festival season, she could be of help to her daughter. They could also give her whatever they could spare of the cash they had in hand.

The couple sat up talking most of the night and finally came to a decision.

Semmi was expected to deliver in a month or so. It would be difficult to take her along. Once she delivered, they couldn't travel with her infant kids either. So they decided to sell her. Poonachi's buck kids weren't strong enough yet. If they grazed for two or three months more, they would find buyers. But there was a high demand for the does right now. They could sell all three.

Once they had come to a decision, the old man asked his wife, 'These kids belong to a special line. Shall we gift one to our daughter?'

The old woman was reluctant. 'Won't she feel bad if we give them away to everyone in the village without giving any to our own daughter? What will her husband and his family think of us?' the old man persisted.

But the old woman firmly rejected the idea. Her daughter

worked tirelessly day and night, and had little children to bring up. The family owned goats and cattle as well. Though they had very little land, the work was endless. How then could she look after a litter of seven kids? The old woman didn't want her daughter to suffer the way she had. She reassured her husband that, in case their daughter expressed any grievance, she would talk to her and manage the situation.

What sense did it make for ordinary folk to own a miracle? Protecting and preserving it was beyond their capabilities. They could see and listen to a miracle, take pleasure in telling others about it, but they couldn't keep it at home and look after it. The problems faced by women in particular were endless. How many lives could her daughter possibly look after? The old woman thought she could explain this to her when they met, and get her to understand.

20

THERE WAS ONLY a month left until their departure for their daughter's village, so the old man figured it would be wise to spread the word right away. He would sell the kids to whoever offered the best price. Since there was heavy competition, they decided not to distinguish between acquaintances and strangers. The villagers would be displeased, so would their acquaintances in the surrounding areas. But it wasn't as though the couple owed them anything. Though everyone wanted a kid, none of them had offered the old man or his wife any help in the past. They'd had to rely on themselves for everything.

While selling an ordinary goat like Semmi involved a visit to the market fair, the old man's strategy was different for the kids. News that he planned to sell the three female kids started in the pasture and spread to the village; from there, it reached everywhere, as fast as the news about Poonachi delivering seven kids had spread at the time. Ten people came by their shed every day. Most of them made it clear that they would buy the kids only if they were given away for free.

'Why, this kid looks like a toddy pot with a head on top, and you're asking such a high price for her,' one fellow said.

'She may deliver seven kids, yes, but will they be goat kids?' another fellow said.

The old man replied patiently to everyone. 'We can't feed them properly,' he said. 'If you give them enough food to fill their bellies, each kid will grow as big as a calf.'

Most of the men who approached him were traders. The old man was wise to their ways. When they wanted to buy something, they would bring down the price as much as possible. Four or five of them would come, one after another, and do it in concert; they would be happy if one of them was able to buy it cheap. They would stick out their bottom lip and leave without a word. They would provoke fear in the seller's mind that the item might never be sold.

The old man understood their tactics. Come what may, he was determined not to sell to a trader. But he kept this to himself. He treated the traders with courtesy. Whenever they threatened him, he acted as though he was afraid. He pretended to be anxious that the kids might never be sold. He provided the traders with variously inflated figures for the expenses he had incurred to raise the kids. He told them he had spent a lot of money on just giving them milk. He whined that he had purchased and provided good feed to the mother goat to make her milk flow. If he was not going to recover even the money he had spent, what was the point of selling the kids, he asked them, weeping in dismay.

The traders were flummoxed. The goatherds were not

given to acting, they knew, and wondered whether the old man was telling them the truth after all. The price quoted by him was indeed very high. The old man knew from experience that this was the only way he could get them to increase their offer. Afterwards, he clammed up and assumed a posture of arrogance. He stood with his face tilted upward, his expression giving nothing away. He asked those who wanted to inspect the kids to come directly to the pasture.

Nothing happened in the first fifteen days after the news had spread through the village and in the vicinity. Now, there were only fifteen days left. The old man was afraid that he might be forced to sell the kids at whatever price he was offered. To worsen his mood, the old woman berated him day in and day out. His strategy was beyond her understanding. She called him 'a greedy monster' and accused him of 'sucking the life out of her by his failure to sell the kids'. As if to prove her right, the traders' visits became less frequent. They were pretending to have lost interest, only to move in for the kill later.

One day, when the old man was seriously wondering whether his approach had been wrong after all, at the hour of dusk when the goats had finished grazing and were about to return home, a man from a distant country appeared in the pasture. His speech and behaviour indicated that he came from an affluent household. The stranger looked the old man up and down, the long loincloth and bare body. Then he looked at the kids. With their bellies full at that hour, they were playing around, butting heads and leaping over one another. The stranger didn't go near them, but he exhaled a sigh, which seemed to indicate a wistful regret that these kids were not growing up in better circumstances. He looked at Poonachi with sympathy.

Then he asked the old man directly, 'Why don't you quote a combined price for the mother and kids?'

'No. Only the three female kids are for sale,' the old man retorted angrily.

'What's your price?' the visitor asked.

The old man quoted his price for the three kids.

'All right, you'll get that price. Why don't you give me the four bucks too, along with the does? I'll pay the same price for each buck kid as I am paying for each doe,' he said.

Only then did the old man realise that the stranger was not some trader who had come to size up the situation. He had come with an objective and a plan. The old man started paying attention to the visitor's words. He had thought that even to sell the buck kids for a normal price, he would have to graze them for two or three months more. Instead, if he was getting the same price for the bucks as for the does, why argue? He decided not to hold the man off with the usual excuse that he would have to consult his wife.

'Take all seven kids together,' he told the visitor.

With his eyes resting on Poonachi, the visitor asked, 'What price are you quoting for the mother?'

'Look at you! You're trying to steal my prime asset. Even if you offer us slabs of gold, my wife would never part with the mother,' the old man said.

But he wasn't really sure. In light of the immense hardships she had suffered while trying to bring up the kids, she might even agree to sell Poonachi, the old man thought. If Poonachi delivered another litter, it would be even more difficult to bring up the kids. So he told the stranger, 'I'll have a word with my wife and let you know.'

The stranger followed close behind the old man, but stopped when they were still some distance away from the couple's home. He asked the old man to call him after he had talked to his wife, and said he would wait there until then. What a civilised person he is, the old man thought. On reaching home, he told his wife about the stranger's proposal even before he had tethered the goats. The old woman found it astonishing too. But she wouldn't agree to sell Poonachi.

'Let's wait for another litter,' she said. This resolve to hold fast to their possessions despite endless difficulties was unique to those who lived off the land. 'Let's wait,' they would say. 'Let's hold on for a few more days.' And they would keep putting off any decision on the matter. This tendency was strong in the old woman too, but she agreed to sell the bucks.

The old man wondered if he should have quoted a higher price.

'Go on! There is no limit to your greed. If we let this deal slip, where can we find a buyer? Call him and say, "You're like God to us. Take these kids with you." No matter how much you give to this heart, it will never be enough.'

'Yes, yes. I forgot. No matter how much you give to this heart, it will never be enough,' the old man laughed.

The buyer read the signal from a wave of the old man's hand and came over. When he was told that the mother was not for sale, he didn't exert any pressure on them. Once the old man had calculated the amount, he paid with a high denomination currency note. The old man didn't have the money to give him the change. 'Keep it,' the buyer told the old man. He could have bought another kid with that amount. The old woman was anxious to return the money. She took all the coins from her pot and brought them to him.

The man said, 'When she delivers the next litter, send word to me. I'll buy one or two kids. Consider this an advance for that purchase and keep it with you.'

His smile made her realise that he meant every word he said. Just then, a cart arrived, drawn by a pair of buffaloes. There were two men in it. They seemed to be servants accompanying the stranger. They got down, caught hold of the kids and put them in the cart. Then they tethered each kid to a peg.

Poonachi was unable to grasp what was going on around her. When she saw her kids being loaded on to a cart, she was distraught; she ran crying towards them. The kids, too, called out feebly to her. With the kids crying from above and Poonachi bleating from below, there was a huge din in the front yard.

'Your daughter says she wants to come to my house, ayah. Why don't you let her?' the stranger said.

'If I let my daughter go, where will I go and beg for milk?' the old woman retorted.

'Just for that reason, you can't keep her at home forever, can you? Being female, she is destined to leave for another home someday,' the man said.

A smooth talker, the old woman thought, but she would not cede the argument. 'She is actually a daughter-in-law who has entered my home, a lady who has come to expand my family,' she said, brimming with pride.

She held on to the rope around Poonachi's neck. Even as the kids kept wailing, the cart started on its way. Poonachi tried pulling at her rope. The old woman brought her to the hut and tied her to a pole. 'Why are you making so much noise? I am also alone here after marrying off my daughter. When a child comes of age, she flies away. We shouldn't worry about it.'

The old woman spoke to Poonachi for a long time. But Poonachi passed the night in a pool of tears. Her family, which had filled the front yard, had vanished without a trace. She had offered her udder and squirted blood for six or seven months to raise them, but what was the use? Not a single kid was left for her to look at. Why did such things happen only to her?

When the kids were around, she had felt sometimes that she might be better off without them. But that stemmed from a feeling of helplessness. For the past few months, being with the kids had become her whole world. There was finally some meaning to her existence. Now it had all come crashing down. Unable to bear her loss, Poonachi cried out. She believed that her cries would reach the ears of her kids, far away in the buffalo cart.

After that day, the old woman didn't say anything at all to Poonachi. She neither scolded her nor tried to discipline her. She preferred to let Poonachi cry her heart out. She would calm down eventually.

The old man was elated. He had a lot of money in his hands. He could spend more than he had foreseen on gifts for his daughter's family. He contemplated some repairs on his tiny parcel of land with the money left.

But first, he had to inform the authorities about the sale of the kids and get the transaction recorded. He decided to take a ride on the buffalo cart with the stranger and his servants. On the way, they chatted a little. Not only were the female kids capable of delivering seven kids at one time, but the buck kids from this line might also be virile enough to father seven kids. The old man understood that this was the buyer's expectation. The buyer's plan was to mate each buck with different females and see whether seven kids would be born in a litter. Let him try it. A man with money can do whatever he wants.

On his way back home after all the work was done, he happened to pass a jeweller's house. For many years, his old wife had been asking him for flower-shaped studs for her ears and a gold chain. He couldn't afford to buy them for her when she was young. But the money newly brought in by Poonachi's kids inspired an extravagance that he had lacked so far. He went into the shop and bought the studs and a gold chain for his wife, along with gold bangles for his daughter, necklaces for his granddaughters and a gold waist-string for his grandson. He still had some money left. In all these years of hard labour, he had never come by so much. He was moved to consider building a temple for Bakasuran.

The old woman was thrilled when she saw the jewellery that her husband had purchased. She tried on the ear-studs and necklace, feeling shy as a bride. She thought of them as gifts from Poonachi and caressed her that night with great affection. The old couple was so overwhelmed by their own good fortune that they were unable to sleep. Grief-stricken at having lost all her kids at one stroke, Poonachi couldn't sleep either.

21

THE JOURNEY WAS nothing like it had been the previous year. There were only four goats left in the herd: Kalli, her two kids and Poonachi. The old man had tied a rope around the necks of the two kids as well. So the couple had to walk holding two ropes each, one in either hand. They never let the goats wander. Even while grazing them, they stood guard on either side. Only after tethering the goats in a spot where plenty of feed was available, did they eat their meals and lie down to rest.

During that journey, the old couple was pleased to discover yet another use for their black goat.

Poonachi had been suckling her kids regularly before they were sold. Now they washed her udder with water every morning and evening, prepared her teats and squeezed milk from them. Poonachi yielded a sombu of milk each time. Only then did they realise that she was of a high milk-yielding breed. Until now, they had never had an occasion to milk her. The old woman had only remembered that Poonachi never had enough milk for her kids. She realised with a start that Poonachi had regularly suckled seven kids.

The couple sold the goat's milk at villages along the way. When this was not possible, they drank a little each and quenched their hunger. The old man had never come across milk that tasted so good, like it had been boiled with jaggery. He forced his wife, who was highly averse to milk, to drink some. This was not milk that gave off a rancid odour; it was the nectar that had been denied to the Asuras. Once the food they had carried with them for the journey got over, it was Poonachi's milk that calmed their hunger along the way. They thought now that Poonachi was indeed a miracle.

Poonachi found the journey extremely dull. It had been highly enjoyable last year. There had been no rope around her neck then. Now there was a long rope tied to a tethering peg at the other end. She could move only as far as the rope permitted her. If she attempted to stray beyond, the rope would immediately pull her back. When there was nobody else around, she tried to bite and mangle the rope with her teeth and get rid of it. But this proved impossible. The old man had twisted and braided agave fibre with his own hands to make the rope. It would only snap if hacked at with a sickle. By the time it wore out and broke on its own, he would have made a new rope.

All the love the couple showed her had shrunk to the length of this rope, Poonachi thought. When the old woman found it difficult to look after the kids, she had freely abused Poonachi. She had called her an evil wretch and a devil. When she got some money from selling the kids, she changed instantly. Now she was carrying all her jewellery

143

in a waist pouch kept hidden under her sari. The couple, who never used to be afraid of thieves, moved about with great caution, in constant fear of being robbed. As soon as she had drunk Poonachi's milk, the old woman would coo fondly to her: 'You are the deity of our clan, Mesayya himself.' Poonachi was wise to all her ways, but what could she do except walk in obedience to the pull of the rope?

All this time, Poonachi never ran short of memories of Poovan. She knew there was no chance of him being alive. By now they would have sold him for meat. Or they would have castrated him and turned him into an inert lump. Who could possibly take his place in her heart? She would have to spend her days in the void of his absence. Neither the route nor her thoughts were pleasant. Poonachi felt a deep loathing for everything.

Meanwhile, during their halt at a village on the way, a villager recognised the old man and asked him, 'Isn't this the wonder-goat that delivered seven kids in a litter?' The old man nodded.

Immediately the man went over to Poonachi, touched her all over and bent down to examine her udder, treating her like an object on display. He also informed the old man that he planned to go into the village and bring a few more people to see the wonder-animal. The old man was immediately struck by an idea. 'There is a charge for touching and looking at the wonder-goat that has delivered seven kids in a litter,' he announced. Accordingly, he started collecting money from visitors. Most of them preferred to gawk at the animal from a distance. He charged a penny each from people who wanted to touch her. But the amount collected was far below his expectation. Poonachi thought the arrangement was good for her. Otherwise, many more would have come and touched her constantly, and taken the life out of her.

In the next few villages, the old man made the same announcement and charged the visitors. The money came in handy for incidental expenses. 'No matter how much you give to this heart, it will never be enough,' the old woman said. 'Correct,' her husband agreed with a laugh.

Contrary to Poonachi's fears, Poovan was still alive. They hadn't castrated him either. His body had bloated and his face looked aged beyond his years. The round face was still the same, but showed faint signs of fatigue. His skin colour had brightened and dazzled the eye. The mole on his face had shrunk to the size of a speck. His horns were long and straight. Porumi was missing, though. They must have sold her or tethered her in a different stall. Poonachi didn't know.

There was a distance of ten feet between Poovan and Poonachi. Nevertheless, she was able to observe him closely. Poonachi's arrival had brought him great joy. At first, he kept glancing at her again and again. Poonachi wondered whether he had failed to recognise her. 'Has my appearance changed all that much?' she thought, scrutinising herself. It was true, perhaps. The last time she came here, she was a little girl who hadn't even come of age. Now she was a nanny goat who had birthed seven kids in a litter, brought them up and lost them all at once. She was weary from having experienced all the sorrows of this world. Could it be that she looked old and worn out? She cried out in an attempt to identify herself. Though her looks had changed, Poovan recognised Poonachi by her voice. It felt to him, in that moment, as though everything he had lost so far had been restored.

Once they had recognised each other, they forgot about the rope around their neck and tugged at it. Poonachi took a long step forward and extended her head. Poovan stuck his head out too and brought his face closer to hers. Their mouths touched each other. Poonachi heard his breathing clearly. Had there been no rope, she would have rested her head on his neck, cried her heart out and eased her pain. When his mouth grazed her puckered lips, she was in raptures, recalling his kisses from the past. 'Why are these goats pulling so hard that the rope might break?' someone said and struck Poonachi on her face. Poovan, too, received a blow. Poonachi stepped back immediately within the bounds of her rope.

Later that morning, they went to the pasture. All the goats of the household grazed together. Both Poonachi and Poovan had a rope that bound their neck and forelegs together. But there was no impediment to their being together. They grazed beside each other all day. Just as he had done the previous year, Poovan pointed her to all the good foliage. Don't we have these plants in our village or is it just that I don't know because there is no one to show me where to find them? Poonachi wondered. Though his neck and forelegs were tied, Poovan lifted a foreleg, raised his head and led her to various spots. While relaxing, they lay down together, their bodies touching. Poonachi felt as if she had told him the whole story of the past year and he had understood it completely.

'I never thought you would be alive,' Poonachi said.

'I didn't think I would stay alive myself. Death can come to a buck kid at any time. We die for meat. We die for sacrifice. I live for moments like these, when I get to be with you, even if only by chance,' Poovan said.

Poonachi replied, 'Do you think a female has it any better? It's better to die than to go through the ordeal of birthing and bringing up kids. I've seen you now. I am not worried about dying anymore.'

They talked about all kinds of things. At dusk, the goatherd drove them back. Though she didn't want to go home, she trudged along reluctantly since Poovan was with her. Seeing the goats go past, the old woman asked her daughter, 'Kannu, do you remember that Porumi we left behind with you? Why is she missing?'

The daughter spoke to her mother in a low whisper: 'Don't ask. My husband's sister came visiting. It seems she told my husband that there was no goat in her house, so he told her she could take one from here. The kid was pregnant and looking very well. I tried protesting that she was a gift from my mother's house. "Don't we need to give my sister a gift from *her* mother's house," he said and laughed. Where could I go and cry about it?'

147

Seeing her daughter in tears, the old woman consoled her and said that such things happened in every household; she must let go of her anger and forget about it.

Porumi's absence made Poonachi very happy. Then it occurred to her that Poovan may have got Porumi pregnant, and she felt dejected. But then, how could she expect that Poovan had remained celibate all these months? It wasn't right, she told herself.

That night, they inadvertently tethered Poonachi and Poovan next to each other. Poonachi felt a profound change in her body. It was the same kind of agony she had experienced a few days after she had parted from Poovan last year. He, too, came alive to the new odour that emanated from her. He approached her in a mood of exultation. There was not the slightest sound from her; no calling out, no cries of agony. He was right next to her, and she gave herself completely to him. Poovan was overjoyed. Poonachi felt him entering her inch by inch. She felt an intense desire to hold him tight and retain him inside her.

Poonachi wished the night would never end. Poovan did all he could to fulfil her desire. He helped her learn the secrets of her own body. He also put her in touch with the novelties of his own. It was a long time before they lay down to rest and even then, sleep eluded them. Poovan kept caressing Poonachi with his tongue and Poonachi reciprocated his affection. Finally they closed their eyes and sank into a deep slumber.

That was when strange noises erupted nearby. All the

goats woke up in fright. There were still several hours to go until dawn. Only Poonachi and Poovan slept on, unknowing.

They came carrying a lamp and woke up Poovan. They undid his tether and dragged him away. Poonachi could only cry helplessly. Recognising that their lives could be in danger, all the goats started bleating. In that confusion, Poovan heard Poonachi's cry. His answering call fell on her ears. What was he saying? Was he telling her, I'll be back soon, don't worry?

No, his voice was laced with the enormous sorrow of parting. His sad cry reached her across the chasm of darkness that lay between them. Where were they taking him at this hour of the night? Did they not like that he was spending so much time with her? Why did people who had nothing to do with them get to decide who should interact with whom and who should stay with whom? Poonachi couldn't go back to sleep. She stood transfixed, looking in the direction Poovan had gone.

Poovan came back in the morning as a lifeless carcass. They had crammed his body into a basket and carried him home. Poonachi saw it only when they tossed it on top of the thatched roof above the front yard. His head was missing. It was lying inside the basket, perhaps.

Poonachi turned her face away. Poovan, who had been alive at night, was a carcass now. Was that the same body that had lured her so powerfully and entered her? How had it happened? They had taken a vow to sacrifice him to Mesagaran. When the festival came to an end, they slaughtered him.

Poonachi sensed from the sounds she heard that his body was being suspended on a hook and skinned. It was a sorrow that surpassed all previous sorrows. She stood still, crying. Sometimes she felt that it was not Poovan's body that hung there: he had become one with her, so how could he still have a body of his own? Now, she was the one who had to look after him. She would protect the one inside her, not allow any damage to his person. He had stayed alive the whole year only so that he could enter her as he had done last night. Once that duty was fulfilled, he left. She was happy that this Mesagaran had permitted them at least that much.

They didn't let the goats go out for grazing the whole day. They tethered them near the fodder pile. Poonachi stood all night gazing at the spot where Poovan had been. She didn't consume even a mouthful of feed. A raw odour entered her nostrils, of Poovan's body being burnt and charred. She inhaled as much as she could of it and held it inside her.

The next two days went by in the same way. Resolving that she must live in order to keep the Poovan inside her alive, Poonachi started nibbling at the fodder. At dawn the following day, the old couple started on their journey home, with Poonachi, Kalli and her kids in tow.

The old woman's daughter told her affectionately, 'You should give me a female kid from Poonachi's next litter. I'll look after her somehow and keep her with me. You shouldn't give me this or that excuse, Amma.'

'I would happily leave Poonachi with you right now. But

let us defer that kind of trouble at least for a while, there's no need for it. I'll keep a kid for you and give it to you when we come next. How can I not give you one?'

The old woman said many things to appease her daughter before she left. As she was leaving, Poonachi had a feeling that Poovan was calling her from behind. She turned instantly and called back in reply. Her call dashed against the neem tree in the front yard and echoed back to her.

22

BY THE TIME the old woman found out that Poonachi was pregnant, she was already two months gone. There was a distinct change in the quantity and quality of her milk and her body had acquired an extra sheen. As the dry matted hair on her skin fell away, new hair sprouted and covered her body.

It was a long time since the old couple had last talked to each other at night. 'How did this Poonachi get pregnant behind our backs? By what miracle can a doe get pregnant without a buck?' the old woman said.

The old man tried to think through various possibilities. Was there ever a doe that came to heat and didn't cry loud enough to summon the whole village? But Poonachi had showed no signs of being in heat. Not a single mating call had been heard. Had she got pregnant on her own? There was no indication that she had become intimate with a buck in the pasture.

Finally the old man guessed the truth: 'She must have got pregnant in our daughter's house when we were there for the festival. Remember, we were so busy we didn't even look at our goats for a whole week.'

Still, the old woman couldn't accept it. There was no proof of how such a thing might have happened. In any case, how could a doe get pregnant without calling out even once? Ordinarily, the calls would be heard for two or three days after the mating, but Poonachi hadn't made a sound. They had no idea how far along she might be. Only the date of delivery would tell them whether she had indeed got pregnant during the pilgrimage. The old woman was waiting for that day.

There was no rainfall that year. People managed somehow with the grain they had saved up. But how would they feed their goats and cattle? Fodder stocks were fast depleting. The old man drove the goats to distant fields for grazing. On all fronts, the situation was dire. Yet, the old woman took proper care of Poonachi. Whatever she could lay her hands on, even if it was a dry leaf, she brought it home. If Poonachi didn't eat it, she put it in the fodder pile thinking that it might come in handy later. With her own money, she bought and fed Poonachi cotton seed and oilcake to give her strength. She would be carrying seven kids, after all.

The old man was hoping for fewer kids in this litter. His wife wished the same too, but she knew that it was not in their hands. She told him that they had to sacrifice a buck kid from the litter to Mesagaran. They should have done it last year, but things had taken a different turn. They had to fulfil two vows now: one kid this year and another in the following year. The old man agreed.

Unlike the first time, Poonachi delivered in the pasture

without any difficulty. The old man was the only one with her. One of the goatherds had alerted him about her condition and he had come running. Everyone in the field rushed there too. They were all keen to witness the spectacle of seven kids being delivered at once. The old man wanted to take Poonachi home. With so many people looking at her, she might be affected by the evil eye. And how could he carry seven infants all the way home?

Poonachi was oblivious to his anxiety. After writhing in pain for some time, she lay down and strained once. The kids slid out and dropped faster than turds. The old man's only job was to wipe the mucus covering over the mouth. Someone volunteered to assist him even in that task. There were no less than seven kids this time as well: five does and two bucks. Two females and one male were pure white in colour. Just like Poovan, all three had a mole on the jaw. Poonachi licked and cleaned all the kids. The old man sent someone home with the news and the old woman arrived with a basket. After that, everything happened as usual.

The ear-piercing official didn't make a personal visit this time. He recorded the births in the office itself. The land was dry and parched due to lack of rain, and survival had become a daily struggle. No one came to look up the kids except a few villagers. For all that, the news spread far and wide through the goatherds. None of the big newspersons turned up, though. Perhaps they had more important news to work on. A miracle was something that happened rarely. If it happened frequently, it was normal.

Two days after Poonachi's delivery, the man who had bought all the kids from her first litter turned up on his buffalo-drawn cart. He looked blankly at the kids, who were stumbling about in the front yard.

He told the old man, 'All the female kids died at different times. I don't know if I didn't look after them properly or it was simply their destiny. I couldn't raise even one of them. The bucks are still around. The goats they impregnated haven't delivered yet. We'll find out then about the number of kids.'

The old man and his wife were sad to hear the news. They had no reason to disbelieve him. It was a terrible disappointment that the man who had paid so much money to buy the kids wasn't satisfied. But why had he turned up this time as well?

The man continued: 'How can we give up on this miraculous line? That's why I've come now. This time around, I'll give them good nourishment right from infancy and raise them myself.'

The couple had been worried about how they were going to manage with seven kids in a drought year. They agreed to sell four of the kids to him. A female kid and a buck, both of whom resembled Poovan, as well as a buck that looked like Poonachi, were retained. The old woman had vowed to sacrifice the black buck to Mesagaran.

This time the old man didn't quote a price for the kids. No matter how much the man pressed him, he simply refused to name a sum. So the man fixed the price himself, paid the due amount to the old man and took the kids away. The amount he paid was well above the market price. When the old man ventured to ask him for his name and the name of his village, he merely smiled.

Poonachi had plenty of milk for her three kids. The pain and agony she had suffered from having to suckle seven kids at the same time was a thing of the past. The old woman didn't have as many goats to look after, either. They had sold Kalli and her three kids. Only Poonachi and her three kids were left.

There was no greenery anywhere. The bare fields stretched all the way to the horizon. The couple didn't take the goats out for grazing anymore. They simply untied Poonachi's tether and let her loose. She went as far as she was able to walk and grazed mostly on grassy bunds.

The kids played all day, merrily climbing, rolling over and jumping on Poonachi. Only now could she experience the pleasure of having little ones. When she looked at the buck and the female kid who resembled Poovan, she felt that he, too, was close to her.

When the kids were three months old, the old man had to go to his daughter's house on some work. He tied a rope around Poonachi's female kid and took her with him. The kid was not even weaned yet. However, the daughter had insisted on it, so she was taken away.

23

ONLY POONACHI AND her two buck kids were left. Memories of Poovan came to her very often these days. One night, it seemed as if he was whispering in her ear and caressing her neck. Instantly, without realising it, she released a cry of longing. She felt the urge to call out all night. The old woman read the signs. 'You want a mate in the middle of a famine, do you?' she scolded Poonachi. But the very next day, she drove Poonachi to the pasture. It was several months since Poonachi had been to the area. It was deserted. Since there was no rainfall, people had sold their goats for any price they could get and reduced their burden.

There seemed to be no goats at all in the pasture, only sheep everywhere. Sheep could survive even by foraging in the dirt. Goats needed a bough of leaves to chew upon. Even so, there was a young buck roaming in the village common. He caught the scent of Poonachi's heat and rushed towards her, screaming. There was frenzy and excitement in his every move. He rubbed against her and tried to bite her all over. He circled around her and nuzzled her with his snout. Poonachi was in no hurry. She watched his antics with relish, like she

157

was looking at a buck from her first litter. Since there were no goats around, no opportunity had come his way before. But today he had found Poonachi.

As Poonachi yielded to all his moves and pleasured him, she couldn't avoid thinking of Poovan. Everyone looked at her and said she was a miracle. But she had looked inside Poovan and found the real miracle. Poovan was a miracle discovered by a miracle: she found it delightful to think of him like that.

The old lady reckoned that Poonachi would deliver any day at the end of five months. After that, she would have to take care of seven kids. She felt giddy just thinking about it. She wondered whether she should have avoided taking Poonachi to the buck. No, that would have been wrong, too. Moreover, if Poonachi had called out continuously for a week or ten days, what would she have done? Where would she have found a buck then? People were trying to sell even young bucks. 'Let Mesagaran show me the way,' she prayed, putting the burden on him.

When the old man came back, she gave him the news. He thought over it for a long time. There was no rain in their daughter's village either, and not a drop anywhere along the way there. 'There has been no rainfall anywhere in the world of the Asuras,' he said. His daughter's family was in dire straits. Not a blade of grass had sprouted in their field. The fodder pile had dwindled to the size of a lean-to. They had sold off most of their goats and cattle. At home, they skipped a meal daily. Only the children were fed something that tasted like gruel. All they did was to look up at the sky, hoping for rain.

He said, 'Everyone is walking with their eyes to the sky. The rain has made even those of us who kept their eyes on the ground look upward.'

His daughter's family wasn't happy at all to receive the female kid. 'Keep her for as long as you can. When you can't anymore, sell her,' the old man told them. In spite of their difficulties, they had invited him to come and stay with them. 'When they are themselves having a hard time, what do we go and do there?' the old man told his wife.

Now that Poonachi was pregnant again, they decided to keep one buck for sacrificing to Mesagaran and sell the other. They couldn't find a buyer, though. The time when meat-sellers came to one's doorstep was over. Even if they were touted as the offspring of a miracle, no one would touch the kids. A few days passed in the expectation that the rich man who had previously bought Poonachi's kids and carried them away in a buffalo cart would come again. Maybe no one had told him, or maybe he wasn't inclined to buy even after he had been told. What could anyone do with a miracle during a famine? Miracles and exhibitions were meant for when people were relaxing after a sumptuous meal.

The call of hunger sweeps aside all other invitations, to rise up in front of you. You become aware of other calls only after you've heeded this one. Even if you're wealthy, you can only eat food, right? A few days later, the old man took the buck to the market fair. There were plenty of goats for sale, but buyers were few, and even they weren't interested in buying goats with money. If they were given away for free, they were ready to drive them home. Normally, a market fair would have different varieties of grains and pulses piled up in abundant heaps. Potential buyers would be summoned with cries and shouts. Now there was nothing at all. The sellers, who were very few, had spread their wares in small heaps. Still, prices were high. The crowd pushed and jostled around them. The old man had never witnessed such a dismal scene in his lifetime.

Holding the kid in his arms, he stood for a long time. Not a single person approached him and asked about the price. Others who had been standing like him began to leave. Another old man who was right next to him said wearily, 'Just buy a measure of rock salt, cure the meat with salt and eat it as junk.' The old man imprinted the neighbour's advice in his mind. There were no buyers at the salt stall in the market. The salt was cheap, though. He collected a measure of salt in his head towel and walked home with the kid in tow.

The market had allowed the old man to understand the state of the world. He began to wonder what would happen if there was no rainfall in the coming year as well. The only thing they could do now was to stay alive till it rained again. He thought furiously about the things he had to do for continued survival. When he reached home, he described to his wife the scenes he had witnessed in the market. She wondered whether the old man was frightening her deliberately. But if there was no one to buy the kid, the situation must be really bad. She didn't understand why he had bought a bundle of salt. 'Only salt is cheap,' he said. 'Are you going to eat the salt?' she asked him.

The next day, the old man began to execute his plan. He asked his wife to let Poonachi suckle the kids. When Poonachi's teats were full of milk, she was to tie the kids up and milk her. For both of them, breakfast that morning was only milk. For lunch they had gruel made from brown millet; at night, a little millet paste. While eating the paste, the old man said, 'We should reduce our intake further to stay alive. Till it rains again, we can skip a meal every day and tie a wet cloth on our belly to keep it cool.'

That night, with his wife assisting him, the old man cut the throat of Poonachi's black buck. It was to be sacrificed to Mesagaran to fulfil their vow. But how could they, at this time, slaughter a goat and throw a feast for the whole village?

He prayed to Mesagaran as he bathed the buck with turmeric water. 'We had tethered this buck just for you. But you are turning this whole world into a heap of dirt. How can I slaughter a goat for you and give a feast? I am offering you the sacrifice here and now. Please give me your consent,' he pleaded with all his heart.

The buck, too, gave his assent by nodding his head and shaking its body. Only then did the old man slaughter it. It was a bright, moonlit night. Unable to do anything, Poonachi looked at the kid's severed head and cried for a while. She recalled the day she had seen Poovan's severed head. 'We die for meat. We die for sacrifice,' he had said. Had her kid died for meat or for sacrifice?

Working carefully, the old man skinned the buck. He cut out the meat and gave it to his wife, who chopped it into small pieces. He squeezed and rinsed the intestines, and carved the head into many pieces. In the end, the kid lay on the palm frond as a heap of mutton. Slowly the old man coated all the pieces with the salt he had bought in the market. By the time they finished the work and went to sleep, the drongos had started calling.

The next day, they climbed the boulder on their field and spread the mutton pieces to dry. Catching the odour of meat, crows and vultures began to circle overhead. The couple planted poles around the boulder and tied pieces of cloth at the top of each pole. Even then, they could not control the crows. They came in droves and struck again and again. The old woman kept a basket upside down on the mutton to protect it from the birds.

Yet, the crows came swooping down. Picking up a big stick, the old man closed his eyes and flung it violently into the air. A crow was hit by the stick and fell down. The old man picked up the bird and hung it from the top of a pole. The other crows cawed from a distance, afraid to come closer. Nevertheless, the old woman scooped up all the pieces of mutton and put them into the basket. More birds entering the fray and fighting for meat seemed to be a portent of greater calamities to come. She brought the mutton safely home without losing even a single piece. Then she spread it out to dry in the front yard. She remained vigilant, though she knew the birds usually hunted in open spaces and tended to avoid homes and the traffic of humans.

As the days went by, they reduced their food intake even further. For breakfast, they had only Poonachi's milk. Even that kept dwindling, since the kids in her belly were growing. At night, the couple drank millet gruel and ate two pieces of junk. On her way to the pasture with Poonachi, the old woman kept stirring up the mud continuously. In some places, she found sedge tubers. She dug them up and collected a handful. It was sufficient to take care of one meal that day.

The old man would leave home early in the morning and go off somewhere. When he came back, he would bring agave tubers, spurge fruit or some other edible item. They went through countless hardships merely to quench their hunger. Their entire stock of junk lasted a month. One night, they butchered Poonachi's other kid and prepared junk out of the meat. They could survive another month somehow. They weren't as badly off as Poonachi, who got nothing.

After squirting the last drop of milk from Poonachi's udder, the old woman stopped milking her, saying that she was likely to yield only blood from now on. There was no blood either, in Poonachi's body. The kids in her belly were sucking that up as well. The fields were bereft of even a small, dry leaf. On some days, Poonachi ate neem leaves or chewed agave plants. Finally, when everything was wiped out, the couple didn't know what to do with her. No one

163

was willing to buy her. If she was given away free, someone would cut her up without bothering about her condition. There were rumours that people were killing and eating cats and dogs.

Every two days, the old man cut one frond from the palm tree on their land. He cut it into tiny pieces and fed them to Poonachi. How could bits of palm frond be sufficient for a heavily pregnant goat? Poonachi was emaciated and looked like a bag of bones. The swell of the kids in her belly was prominent. Once the kids are delivered, I can bury them in a pit and slaughter Poonachi for meat, the old man thought. His wife wouldn't agree. 'I'm ready to bury her, but I'll never allow her to be slaughtered for meat,' she said, raising her voice.

'Ever since this cursed thing entered our house, she has cleaned out all the live animals from here. Now she will wipe out the humans too, just wait and watch,' the old man cursed her.

24

THERE WERE NO goats, cattle, poultry, cats or dogs in any house in the village. People were desperate, not knowing what to do. Some families left for other villages and towns. When the entire land of the Asuras had not received a drop of rain, what was the point of going anywhere? Once every week, government officials distributed a kilo of flour to every household for cooking gruel. It wasn't sufficient for even a single meal. People were desperate to get the flour, however. Going to the supply point, standing in a queue and collecting the flour proved to be a real ordeal. 'Queue up, queue up,' the assistants kept yelling. Even then, how could they give up what was being given to them? There were rumours that in a few days, the government was going to open one gruel stand for every five or six villages.

The couple were worried about how their daughter was coping. They knew that visiting her would only add to the family's burden, and seeing them suffer first-hand would be unbearable. If someone was going to their village, the couple would ask them to find out about the family's welfare.

The old man tried to sell a set of pots from the house,

but he could find no buyers. To start with, he sold the ear-studs and chain that he had bought from the sale of Poonachi's kids and brought back whatever money he could get for them.

The only copper and brass items they had were a couple of small bowls and a sombu. He sold these at the market fair and bought half a measure of pearl millet with the money. His wife put the grain away safely, intending to give it to Poonachi after her delivery. The old man didn't like his wife to do anything extra for Poonachi. He only wanted to sell or dispose of her; he just couldn't figure out a way.

Poonachi was beset by a ravenous hunger. She was constantly famished. The green fronds were not enough. She ate the bark off trees. With great effort, she chewed and swallowed sticks and twigs. She couldn't even fill her belly with water. The old woman trudged to some distant place and came back carrying a pot of water. From the pot, she would measure out a little water and give it to Poonachi.

Poonachi's other problem was the load in her belly. The kids weren't getting enough nourishment. They lay inside her, wriggling like worms. Each kid kicked in a different direction. Poonachi's spine and ribs showed as lines on her body; her lower abdomen hung down like a bag.

Poonachi didn't have the strength to carry her stomach and walk. She couldn't stand for even a few minutes. There was no option but to lie down often, but getting up was very hard. She had to push her body forward, kneel with her forelegs bent, lift her hindquarters and get up. Since her forelegs lacked the strength to support her, they would buckle and fold. After getting up halfway, she would drop suddenly to the floor. Unable to bear its own weight, her stomach would dash against the ground and Poonachi could feel her kids squirming and crying. By the time she got up, she felt as if she had been to the brink of death and back.

One day, after lying down for a while, Poonachi wanted to get up. Her legs had turned numb and wooden. She had to stretch to set them right. If she couldn't even unfold them from a bent position, what could she do? She tried several times to lift herself up. She could raise her body slightly, but her legs wouldn't cooperate. She hadn't stood up for so long that they had become immobile. Poonachi cried feebly. She couldn't even raise her voice now. It was as weak as it had been when she was an infant.

When the old woman's eyes happened to fall on Poonachi, she realised that she was crying. She ran to her and assisted her by lifting and holding up her lower body. Poonachi could not plant her numb legs firmly on the ground. The old woman massaged her limbs until life returned to them.

After that incident, whether it was day or night, the old woman remained vigilant. Every now and then, she would lift Poonachi and make her stand. Soon it came to pass that Poonachi could not get up without the old woman's help. The old woman too became despondent and fearful, wondering how Poonachi was going to deliver her litter and what they were going to do with the kids. There were very few palm fronds left on the tree. Now they were forced to snip the sprouts. All the fences in the fields had dried up and collapsed. There was only bare soil everywhere. Would they have to eat dirt from now on?

The old woman took out the millet grain that she had planned to give Poonachi after the delivery. She ground a fistful and cooked some gruel with the flour. These were the very last bits of grain in the house. The couple drank a mouthful each and went to sleep.

The old woman's belly had shrunk and her body was weak. When she lay down, she fell asleep at once. She had laid her cot right next to Poonachi. Before she lay down to sleep, she lifted Poonachi and got her to stand up. Poonachi's legs trembled as if they were going to snap and collapse any minute. Still, she made an attempt to stand. She wished each day that the load in her belly would reduce. How were these kids growing inside her merely on pieces of palm frond? The weight was unbearable.

Wanting to lie down, she bent her forelegs slowly and planted her knees on the ground. Suddenly her body slid to the ground, lacking even its usual strength. She felt her consciousness disconnecting from her body. She rested her head on a side post of the hut. She needed support of some kind. Thoughts raced chaotically through her mind.

She had no memory of the time she had spent in Bakasuran's arms. She knew about it only through the old man's ebullient description of their meeting. The scene embedded in her mind as her first memory was that of the old woman cooing 'Poonachi, Poonachi' and putting her on her lap. Though she suffered for want of milk, those days were quite pleasant. Enraptured by her memories, Poonachi fell asleep. Different faces came to her in her dreams. Poovan appeared most often. The face of every kid she had ever birthed appeared too. The obese shape of the old ram that had tried to mount her in the big pen crept in like a shadow and engulfed her. The figure of Bakasuran formed inside her and grew. He was as tall as a palm tree. His arms hung down like thin sticks. He placed Poonachi on the tip of his finger, lifted her up, and gently moved the finger in circles. Poonachi felt giddy. Circling faster and faster, he flung her into space. Poonachi rose up in the air and fell upside down towards the ground. Her heart was racing. Her face would be smashed to bits like a coconut when she hit the earth. That would be the end of her. Right now. Poonachi opened her eyes suddenly.

It was dark all around. Her head was resting on the side post of the hut. She shook her head. It hadn't hit the ground yet. It was still intact. She felt dizzy. It seemed as if her whole body had become numb, as if she had been lying down for a long time. Captivated by her dreams, she had lost track of time. Perhaps the old woman would come and lift her up. What had happened to her?

She looked at the cot, her eyes now accustomed to the darkness. The old woman lay inert. Poonachi tried to raise her voice and call out to her. The night was bereft of sound. The chatter of birds had died down a long time ago. There were no cries of goats or cattle, no chirping of insects or beetles either. Everything seemed to have frozen still.

Poonachi tried to raise her voice. A feeble sound emerged from her throat. She kept trying. It didn't look like the old woman was going to get up. She couldn't move her own body at all. Nothing seemed to be moving inside her belly, either. Was there no movement, or was she incapable of sensing it? Her body turned hard as a stone and sank into the dirt. Only her consciousness was still alive. She rested her head again on the side post. It refused to stay up, and kept sliding down. She tried with all her strength to settle back on the post. After that, she had no idea what happened.

When the old woman woke up in a panic and checked, Poonachi seemed to be asleep with her head drooping to one side. The old woman ran to her urgently and touched her.

What lay there was not Poonachi, but a stone idol.

Translator's Note

IT IS A LITERARY translator's lot, as well as privilege, to work with texts that cover a range of milieus, time periods and genres. The one thing common to all these texts is that the worlds they describe are inhabited mostly by humans. In contrast, the world of animals is normally a staple of children's literature. I haven't had the opportunity – or, truth be told, the inclination – to engage, as a translator, with works of creative fiction for children. *Poonachi, or the Story of a Black Goat* features animals that think and feel, but it is not a novel meant for children. In fact, it may be the first Tamil novel about animals written for adult readers. George Orwell's *Animal Farm* (1945) and Mikhail Bulgakov's *Heart of a Dog* (1925) are two famous examples of this genre and readers who are familiar with the genre would not be far off the mark if they expect *Poonachi* to be an intensely political work like these two texts.

We live in dark times where our most intimate human feelings, as they have evolved through the ages, are under siege. We are compelled to protect and assert their primacy in order to stay human and sane. In *Poonachi*, Murugan has done a marvellous job of creating a narrative that takes a feeble goat through a range of basic human emotions and urges. As we track the destiny of this orphan goat, shaped by a force-field of humans and animals, we realise that the author's real theme is our own fears and longings, primordial urges and survival tactics. Through a feat of storytelling that is both masterly and nuanced, Murugan makes us reflect on our own responses to hegemony and enslavement, selflessness and appetite, resistance and resignation, living and dying. *Poonachi* is not just the story of a goat. Through his exploration of the life journey of an animal, Murugan leads us deep into 'an intimate history of humanity' and the irreducible human essence that we must fight to preserve.

Starting life as a foundling and going through the ordeal of being a miracle, Poonachi experiences both the promise and the structural violence embedded in the life of a female. In Murugan's tale, she turns into a stone idol at the moment of her death, harking back to a hoary tradition in the folk culture of Tamil Nadu whereby the memory of an innocent girl destroyed by the random and ever-present violence of the world is worshipped as a deity. And this may well be the key to reading this novel as an adult literary text for our times.

As a translator, it was a novel experience for me to work with a narrative in which the feelings and experiences of animals, and the countless manifestations of their physicality, are tracked and described with subtlety and flair. I hope a close reading of the text will lead the reader to discover and recognise herself in and through Poonachi's world and the tribulations of her brief, pain-filled existence.

My grateful thanks to V.K. Karthika, my editor at Westland, for the grace, skill and diligence with which she has edited this complex text. Needless to add, the errors that remain are mine.

N. Kalyan Raman
Chennai
25 December 2017